THE STORE
THAT MAMA BUILT

THE STORE THAT MAMA BUILT
Robert Lehrman

MACMILLAN PUBLISHING COMPANY

NEW YORK

MAXWELL MACMILLAN CANADA

TORONTO

MAXWELL MACMILLAN INTERNATIONAL

NEW YORK   OXFORD   SINGAPORE   SYDNEY

While this story is clearly based on family stories, and while Harrisburg and Steelton are real places, *The Store That Mama Built* is fiction. Though I've tried to square the story with historical events, I have taken liberties with the geography of Steelton, and have invented most incidents. Furthermore, the emotions and prejudices of these characters arise out of my imagination and are not to be ascribed to any real people, living or dead.

Macmillan Publishing Company is part of the
Maxwell Communication Group of Companies.
Macmillan Publishing Company
866 Third Avenue
New York, NY 10022
Maxwell Macmillan Canada, Inc.
1200 Eglinton Avenue East
Suite 200
Don Mills, Ontario M3C 3N1
First edition
Printed in the United States of America

1 3 5 7 9 10 8 6 4 2

The text of this book is set in 11 pt. Sabon.

Library of Congress Cataloging-in-Publication Data
Lehrman, Robert.
The store that Mama built / Robert Lehrman. — 1st ed.
p.   cm.
Summary: In 1917 twelve-year-old Birdie and her siblings, the children of Jewish immigrants from Russia, help their recently widowed mother run the family store, picking up where their father left off in his struggle to succeed in America.
ISBN 0-02-754632-2
[1. Jews—Fiction. 2. Emigration and immigration—Fiction.
3. Russian Americans—Fiction. 4. Stores, Retail—Fiction.] I. Title.
PZ7.L53275St 1992   [Fic]—dc20   91-39983

*To my beloved uncles and aunts,
Joe (1900–1962), Jack, Bert,
Rose, and Gert—
and my father, Harry—
whose detailed reminiscences
stimulated and enriched this book.*

One

Her sobs were so loud they began drowning out the rabbi, even from where I stood. And when the grave diggers, burly Irishmen in work clothes who had taken off their caps out of respect, picked up the pine coffin, Aunt Annie hurled herself on it. She pressed her face against the untreated wood, embracing as much of it as she could with her arms, as if keeping the coffin above ground would somehow keep Papa alive.

Everybody stood still for a second, not knowing what to do. Two of my uncles went over to her. One of them bent down and whispered something. Then each of them took an arm and, gently but firmly, lifted her up and led her, stumbling, off down the grassy slope of the cemetery hillside.

It was April, 1917. Three days before, Papa had died of influenza in Steelton, a little town outside Harrisburg, Pennsylvania, where we had been living for four months: Mama; Papa; my three brothers, Joe, Jack, and Harry; my two sisters, Rose and Gert; and I. For the funeral we had come back up to New York, where most of the family lived, immigrant Jews who had come over from Russia during the last three decades.

I was a skinny twelve-year-old with thick, wavy brown hair and the wide cheekbones that made people tell me I looked just like Mama. I was the only one of the girls old enough to be allowed at the funeral. I knew I shouldn't feel good about anything at my father's funeral, but that made me feel special, nevertheless. Two years before, when Mama's sister Ida had died, only the boys had gone.

I stood, not crying, trying to look somber, like Mama, who stood without expression beside me, a few feet from the open grave. My three brothers stood on the other side, along with Bubba, Papa's mother.

Bubba was a stern-looking old lady. At her apartment a few hours before, while everyone was dressing for the funeral, I had gone into her bedroom and gotten a shock. Bubba was sitting at her dresser without her *sheitl*, the black wig she always wore. Her real hair was white and short and thin, with great patches of pink scalp shining through. She looked frighteningly old.

Bubba wasn't crying, either. I thought it must be because she was used to these things. She had given birth thirteen times, but only eight of her kids were alive. Seven, with Papa gone.

But why wasn't *I* crying? Shouldn't I be more like Aunt Annie, thinking only of Papa, instead of watching like a reporter and letting my mind wander to the silliest and most irrelevant things—how bare the trees were, and how if you listened carefully you could hear the screech of trains traveling along the El a few blocks away?

Afterward, when we were all walking up the gravel path of the cemetery toward the hired cars that would take us back to Brooklyn, another one of my father's sisters came up to us. She was the sister who lived in New Jersey. Almost everybody was going back to Bubba's

8

apartment after the funeral to sit *shiva*, the Jewish way of mourning the dead. But she had to go right back to work. She fished an envelope from the pocket of her full black skirt. "Birdie," she said.

My English name was Bertha. When I was little the closest I could come to that, they tell me, was Birdie. Now everybody called me that, even Bubba.

"Yes, Aunt Yettie."

"I want you to have this," she said in Yiddish.

I took the envelope. Inside was a postcard with Russian writing on it, and on the picture side a photograph of a young boy, very serious, standing with a younger-looking Bubba.

"Papa when he was a boy," Mama said to me, also in Yiddish.

"Girls save these things," Bubba said. "When she's my age, it'll be on the wall."

I barely heard her. I had stopped walking and was staring down at the picture, stunned. I had never seen a picture of Papa as a boy, or dreamed that one existed. And suddenly I burst into tears.

All three women stopped walking and bent down. *"Mein perele, mein perele,"* Mama said—my little pearl.

"Oy, she misses her papa," Bubba said, not in a stern voice at all. Glancing up, I saw that Aunt Yettie actually smiled; maybe she was pleased that her gift had had an effect.

We had gone to Harrisburg because Papa's two uncles, Isadore and Raphael, were there. Izzie had a general store, and Raphael had a clothing store. Papa was confident that with work and luck he could do at least as well.

But when we first moved he started out as a peddler.

He used to take a horse and wagon and go out into the countryside, buying things from farmers—a hunk of metal, a wheel, a butter churn—and selling them to junk dealers back in the city.

Papa was a short man with a head full of dark, curly hair, and he was quick to anger. Once in New York he had picked up a stick and hit a business partner over the head for beating a horse. Even after more than twenty years in America he didn't speak English well, although he spoke it much better than Mama did. So in the house we spoke Yiddish. But the farmers thought his accent was cute. They liked his little jokes. And they liked his prices. After a few months he started selling coffee and spices out of a wagon. He would just go up and down the streets of Harrisburg, shouting out his wares. Within days he was selling more than he ever did to junk dealers. There were nights when, after he had come home, he would sit at the kitchen table counting his receipts for the day, separating the bills, making piles out of the silver coins or the occasional gold one. He would look up at us. *"Aruf arbeten,"* he would say—we're on the way up.

When he had come to America, the first thing he had done was shave his beard, but he was still religious. He got up each morning before anyone, put on his silk tallis and his phylacteries—black leather cubes containing scriptural passages and worn during weekday prayer on the arm and forehead by Orthodox Jews. Then he would stand, praying for an hour, until it was time for the boys to get up. His uncles in Harrisburg were Reform, but he had joined the Orthodox shul. Each Friday night and Saturday morning we would walk there, a mile each way, for services.

None of us liked it. To me the congregation praying

10

sounded like a swarm of bees, buzzing softly, then loudly, in Hebrew, a language only the boys were allowed to understand. Occasionally the rabbi, a man about Papa's age, whose moist lips poked through a beard glistening with spittle, would announce a page number. The voices would swell into a familiar tune, then subside into the drone again, broken only by the flapping sounds of pages being turned.

If I endured it, though, the boys hated it. This was especially true for Joe and Jack, seventeen and fifteen, who parted their hair in the middle, wore long pants—not knickers—and neckties to school, and had been seen smoking cigarettes on a downtown street. They both could have had jobs on Saturday if Papa had let them work.

"*Shabbes* is a day of rest," he had said.

"Why should God care if we're resting?" Joe said.

"I can pray while I sweep floors," Jack said. "I know everything by heart."

"If you know by heart, you already know my answer."

I was sitting in the living room, marveling at their audacity and disappointed by their lack of respect at the same time. How would they answer that?

But they didn't. They didn't want to win. It was daring enough to argue. "Well, okay," Jack said. They worked each afternoon after school and on Sunday, since in Pennsylvania stores stayed open on the Christian Sabbath.

Their only victories were in small things—for example, on Friday nights, Papa would turn to Joe and say "Yussel, for wine, you say the *broche*?"

Joe would seem to be considering saying the prayer,

then turn to Heshie, our name for Harry, whose Hebrew name was Herschel. "Ah," he'd say, "let Heshie do it."

If his shrug was a little too careless, Papa might say, "No, you do it. Please." Then Joe would have no choice. But if he did it just right, if there was the merest pause, as if he recognized the honor and was feeling generous enough to pass it on, we would see Papa decide to swallow his annoyance. "Okay. Fine. Heshie, would you be good enough?"

But these were skirmishes, minor rebellions. Both boys looked up to Papa. The fact was, with the three of them working, we had more money than ever before.

Then one day—this was in 1916—Papa decided he was ready for the next step. He came home that night, smiling through dinner as if at a private joke. Then, at one point, using English even though Mama was sitting there, he told us he had a surprise for us. "How you like to leef in a beeger howze?"

It turned out he had already found one, and had had Uncle Izzie go by to look: a little corner house in the town of Steelton, built around the steel mills outside Harrisburg. The front of the house had been a grocery store a few years back, and it could be one again. There was a big window in the front room. The counter and glass showcases were still there. Then, if you went through a short hallway, you came to a kitchen. Past the kitchen were a living and dining room, and a fair-sized room where Gert, Rose, and I could all sleep. Upstairs were three more bedrooms.

The place was run-down. There was termite damage to the floors, and there were holes in the ceilings. But Papa was impressed by something Uncle Izzie had pointed out: Opening a store in this town would make us the only grocery for almost a mile in all directions.

It was mid-December when we moved in. And during that winter, while we got used to our new schools, Papa worked doubly hard. By day he worked on the coffee route. At night he and the boys worked on the house. They laid a new floor in the front room. They painted and plastered. For weeks we kept windows open to get rid of the smell of fresh paint. We borrowed some money from Papa's uncles and put in more showcases, and we bought a new coffee grinder, which meant we could grind and bag coffee to sell in the store.

We were as excited about the house as Papa was. We had even liked Harrisburg. It had taken us only a month or so to realize how lucky we were to be there and to have escaped New York. On Floyd Street in Brooklyn, where we had lived, along with most of my father's brothers and sisters and their families, the apartments were tiny. The six of us had slept in two beds, the boys in one, the girls in another. In winter that meant we fought for blankets. In the summer, when it was so hot you sat outside on the steps fanning yourself until bedtime, you would put off going in until the last possible moment, because when you went inside the heat would slam into you as soon as you began climbing stairs. Then, in bed, with bodies next to you, you would feel sweat trickling down your cheeks and jaw even if you lay still.

In New York the buildings were full of roaches. We saw them crawling up walls and over the pipes. No matter how many times we scrubbed the bathroom floor with lye, we would see them a few hours later, racing alongside the tub or disappearing through tiny cracks in the molding. When it was dark they would cluster on the floor in the kitchen, darting underneath the stove if you turned on the light.

The places people worked were terrible, too. Uncle

13

Max, my father's older brother, owned a knitting mill in Brooklyn. It was actually a storefront with space that went way back to the other end of the building. Greasy knitting machines lined both sides of a long, single aisle. Naked light bulbs hung down on long wires from the ceiling. The place smelled of sweat and grease, and there were as many roaches there as we had in the apartments.

A lot of our relatives worked in Uncle Max's mill. They worked from seven in the morning till seven at night making sweaters. One day Mama and I stopped in at the place, walking from front to back. Mama was smiling and patting the back of each cousin we passed, bent over spools of colored yarn, but after we got outside she shook her head. "You'll never catch me doing that work," she said.

Harrisburg was different. We lived in a house right from the day we moved, on Hanna Street, a block from the Susquehanna River, which ran through the town. During the day we could hear the whistles from the coal boats moving slowly north. There was a concrete walkway beside the river. In nice weather you could walk along it or play in a park lined with trees. Our relatives had stores and lived in houses with yards in back, and white birch trees in front.

Mama didn't like Steelton as much as Harrisburg. It was close to the mills, and sometimes ash from the tall, brick smokestacks—red from the iron, somebody told us—would cover the streets, and the bottoms of our shoes would be red.

But some days you just wanted to sit and watch as flame and sparks sprayed from the smokestacks. Besides, the new house was even bigger than the first one. Papa put dividers in the two bedrooms, bought a few extra beds, and suddenly Joe could sleep alone and so could I. Occasionally we would see a cricket. Before Mama scrubbed the place, there were spider webs and eggs in the corner of each dusty window. But for some reason, roaches didn't live there—even when there was food around. Who wouldn't like it?

One day in late March, Papa had a sign painter come. On that front window, with gold paint, the painter brushed on the letters: L. FRIED: GROCERIES.

It had been a cold winter. The branches on the trees were still black and bare. But when the painter was done we all gathered out in front, not bothering with coats, to look at it. Inside the window Jack had put up a sign that said OPEN SOON.

Papa put his arm around Mama. She squirmed away; she never liked public displays of affection. But he squeezed her against him. *"Aruf arbeten,"* Papa said.

A week later, he started coughing. They took him to the hospital. There was a big flu epidemic that year, though not as big as the one the year after. Nowadays flu is no big deal. But back then, you could die from it. And he died.

Gert was five and Rose seven; Mama left them behind with Uncle Izzie. She took the three boys and me up to New York for the funeral. On the same train, a few cars back, was Papa's body.

TWO

It was a trip we made in silence, early in the morning. We would take the coffin to our old synagogue in Brooklyn for the service, then go with it to the cemetery late that same afternoon. The train clacked its way past the dark brick warehouses and factories north of Harrisburg, through towns and past farms and along the curving banks of the river. Mama, Jack, and Joe sat together, seeming too stunned to talk. I sat with Heshie, who was reading, once in a while putting the book face down on the hard wicker seat and staring out the window.

I was as quiet as everyone else. I tried to look stricken. The trouble was, though I knew it was horribly selfish, I was having a hard time keeping my mind on Papa's death. What I found myself thinking about most of the time was whether we would stay in Steelton or move back to New York, which Mama had hinted she wanted to do.

Oh, I knew her reasons, all right. Jack had explained them to me. She liked Izzie, but he and Raphael were on Papa's side and not to be counted on like your own flesh and blood. She was scared of opening the store. She was scared of what would happen to Joe and Jack. Sure, they could leave school and get full-time work. But she wanted them to finish and maybe even go to college. At seventeen,

Joe was almost ready. He was taking bookkeeping in school and had told her he wanted to be an accountant.

And what about the rest of us? Somehow she had to make a living in order to feed four more kids who wouldn't all be out of the house for another fifteen years. How was she going to do that, a thirty-nine-year-old woman who spoke English only when she had to?

But to leave Pennsylvania! To leave a house where I could get into my bed at night and stretch my arms out knowing I wouldn't bump up against one of my sisters! To go back to a place where you had to crane your neck out of the kitchen window even to see a postage-stamp-sized patch of blue sky!

There had to be a better way, and the only trouble was, though I could never tell this to anybody, I didn't trust Mama to make the right decision.

After all, even a twelve-year-old could see it had always been Papa who would decide when we moved and where we would live. Meanwhile, Mama would spend the entire day cooking and cleaning and making sure that everything was the way Papa liked it.

This was the way it was for people who had been born in the old country, and Mama was very definitely from the old country. Although we would never tell her, we were embarrassed by how little she knew.

Once we all went to a Fourth of July concert at a band shell down by the riverbank in Harrisburg. We came home singing some of the songs we had heard, including "Yankee Doodle."

"What does that mean, 'doodle'?" she asked when we were done.

"Mama," Joe said, laughing, "how long you been in this country? Twenty years?"

"Twenty-four."

"You never heard that song?"

"The song I heard. The meaning I didn't hear. I never heard the word 'doodle.' "

"It's just a nonsense word."

"Nonsense?"

"Makes no sense. It means nothing."

"Oh."

"It's just a funny song," I said.

"Foolish, if you ask me," she said.

When we went out for a walk or to a movie and ran into Sophie Weingarten from school with her parents, both of them born in America, Mama would smile and say nothing and let Papa do all the talking, like some peasant woman who didn't understand a word.

"Why didn't you say anything?" I asked one time, trying to make it sound as if I were just curious.

"I did. I said hello."

She had said it in Yiddish. "But, Mama, they probably think you just speak Yiddish."

She looked at me, smiling in a way that I knew meant she was hurt. "I let Papa do the talking. Why not?"

I knew this was wrong, but I couldn't find the words to tell her why. "Because you do speak English," I said.

"When I have to."

Her placid acceptance of this was never more infuriating than on *Shabbes*. On Fridays, Mama would usually do a double cleaning, scrubbing the walls, preparing a meal of chicken and vegetables and *zemels*—sweet rolls filled with raisins and cinnamon. Especially once we had moved to Steelton, where the synagogue was even further away than it had been in Harrisburg, we would have dinner ready to serve the instant Papa came home, so we could have an hour before it was time to leave.

18

As the oldest girl I was responsible for cleaning, and Mama set me to work as soon as I came in from school. I loved my sisters and brothers, but I would seethe as I mopped the floor and dusted every windowsill while my two sisters made mud pies and the boys played kick-the-can in the street.

"Why can't the boys help?" I asked once, a few weeks after we had moved to the new house.

Mama smiled. "They work hard. They're putting in that new floor."

"Still. They're not doing it now."

She paused, cupping her hand and making a little pile of the carrot scrapings collecting on the chopping block. "Girls do some things and boys do others."

"Girls do all the work," I said.

That night, after we had lit the *Shabbes* candles and said the prayers over the wine and bread, Mama jumped up, motioning to me to come into the kitchen to help serve.

I pretended not to notice. Out of the corner of my eye I could see her staring at me, leaning forward to scrape up a little wax that had fallen from the candles onto the table. Then she went in and began serving without me.

I still cleaned—she expected that. But after that she didn't ask me to help serve dinner.

Well, why volunteer for something so clearly unfair? I didn't, not even on the horrible first night after Papa's death, when Izzie and Raphael's wives brought over food, and we were packing for the trip north, and Mama was sitting on the couch crying constantly. Nobody expected me to; the wives took over the kitchen. But I knew I could have helped, and afterward I was ashamed that something had made me hang back.

19

It even occurred to me that I would be punished for it by what was going to happen in New York. Because now I was sure I knew what would happen. As we'd boarded the train, I had heard Jack tell Joe that Uncle Max might urge Mama to move to New York and take a job in the mill.

"That stupid place?" I burst out. "Mama hates that place."

"Life isn't all pleasure, Birdie," Jack said.

Instantly I knew it was true. I had sounded like a little kid. But as we took our seats and looked out the windows, I hated Uncle Max, who had always picked me up and planted kisses on my head and quarters in my pockets, and who, when we'd toured the plant, would give me for toys stacks of the cylindrical cones on which the yarns were wound. And, shameful as it was, I was angry at Mama because I was sure she would say yes.

But wasn't it horrid of me to think about this at all? Shouldn't we sit quietly, think sad things about Papa, and keep a somber expression on our faces so that even strangers would know we had had a tragic loss? Even looking out the train window seemed wrong because to see us move along, picking up speed, made the trip feel too much like an adventure.

Heshie was reading *The Last of the Chiefs*, by Joseph Altsheler, his favorite writer. All the boys read Altsheler books. I had never read any of them. From the way Heshie described them, I knew I would find them disgusting: books about fighting Indians or fighting in the Civil War, books full of battle scenes and caves to hide in and great cliffs off of which people jumped into the rapids below.

Heshie was fourteen, and I liked him best of the boys because he sometimes let me tag along with him even when he was with a friend. Sometimes he even let me go along when he was doing what he loved best: going to William S. Hart movies—cowboy movies—at the Palladium theater. I didn't like these movies any better than Altsheler books. I went because of the honor of it.

Usually I could talk to Heshie, but now he looked like he didn't want to be disturbed, especially after the first half hour, when he seemed so caught up in his reading he forgot to look upset. I let him read until we were past Philadelphia, when he put the book down on his lap. "Good story," he said.

"Did you read it already?"

"Nah." He began telling me about it. This one was about two brothers whose wagon train got attacked by Indians. Where he was up to, they had just found a valley and an abandoned hut built by beaver trappers, and they were going to "ride out" the winter.

"I guess I don't feel like reading," I said, more loftily than I'd intended.

"Because of Papa?"

"Yeah."

"Boy, just because you read a book doesn't mean you don't care. You think I don't care, Birdie?"

"I didn't say that."

"I care, Birdie. Just, this takes my mind off it."

I realized I had accused him of something terrible. Grateful that he hadn't railed at me for it, I changed the subject, bringing up something else that was on my mind. "Will they let us see the body?" I asked.

"When I went to Aunt Ida's, the watchamacallit, the casket, was open."

"Did you see her?"

"Yeah. She looked like a mummy."

"I don't want to see Papa."

"Don't you want to say good-bye?"

A wave of sadness swept over me, the way it did whenever I heard certain words: good-bye, death, parents. "Sure I do. But you don't need to see his body to say good-bye. What's in his body? A telephone right to heaven?"

"No. But people want to do it. Unless it's scary. Are you scared?"

"Why should I be?"

"Because little kids, they don't realize people die."

"I'm not a little kid."

"I don't mean you, Birdie. I mean real little, like Rose or Gert."

I nodded to show I had forgiven him. "Do you think Papa will go to heaven?"

"No, I don't."

"You don't think he was a good man?"

"I don't think there is a heaven. It's a story, like Santa Claus for the Christians."

"Papa believed."

"Believed in God, yeah. But not in heaven."

"Do you? In God, I mean."

"Yes."

"Well, if there's no heaven, where does God live?"

That stumped him. He thought for a second, then nodded a few times, smiling. "I don't know." He shrugged and smiled to show that I had a good point and he wasn't offended that I had made it. "I just don't know."

He didn't know! How often could I get one of the boys to admit ignorance? But I felt uncomfortable pursuing this further. I didn't know if I believed in heaven, either. After all, if there *was* one, how far up was it? Hadn't we just learned that the solar system went on for billions of miles? Of course, if Papa had believed it I would have felt as if I should, too, if only out of respect for the dead. But if Papa *didn't* believe it—and Heshie should know—then why should I?

A whistle blew, a long and two short ones, and the train went by a crossing. Two open cars sat there. The people inside were dressed up, the men wearing hats. Behind them was a horse and wagon. It looked like the horse was scared by the train; the driver was shouting at it and jerking on one sweat-darkened rein.

"Will you stay at Bubba's?" Heshie asked.

There wasn't enough room for us all in one apartment, but it wasn't clear how the relatives would split us up. "I think so."

"Where?"

"Prob'ly on the couch."

"That's good."

"I don't like staying there," I said, and realized this was a clue to my secret thoughts. I flushed, wondering if he could tell.

"Me, neither. The *roaches*."

"But it's nice seeing everybody."

"Yeah, well, I'm scared we'll be seeing them too much."

Even before I heard another word, my heart began to beat as if I had a secret deformity and had just discovered somebody else had it, too. "Why?"

"Mama's gonna want to live with Aunt Esther, and probably Uncle Max, he'll say work in the mill, and we'll never go back to Steelton except to pack up."

"You worry about *that*?"

"Practically every minute. I know I shouldn't. I can't help it."

At that moment I felt such gratitude that I could have

reached over and hugged my brother. "I'm thinking about it, too."

"I don't mean I'm not thinking about Papa. I think about Papa a lot."

"Oh, me, too. But I don't want to go back to New York."

"I hate the damn place."

"Don't swear, Heshie."

"Well, I do."

"I do, too. But we shouldn't talk about it now. It's selfish."

He smiled. "You think it means we're not good people?"

"Maybe."

"Ah. That's the way people are, Birdie. Besides, know what?"

"What?"

He leaned forward and whispered, "I bet that's what's on Mama's mind, too."

Three

After the funeral, all of us except Aunt Yettie got into a caravan of rented cars and went back to Bubba's house, on a street lined with walk-up apartment buildings on both sides. This was where we had lived before moving to Pennsylvania, and where Bubba had lived with my grandfather until his death.

When we arrived, the cousins who hadn't gone to the cemetery met us with pitchers of water and towels as we got out of the cars. I had never seen this before. Mama saw I was puzzled. She told me it was a custom; we were supposed to let them pour the water over our hands, say a prayer, then wipe with the towel. This would wash away the pain of death. It sounded silly to me, and I saw Joe roll his eyes. But I let them do it.

We went upstairs, where chairs had been pulled away from the dining-room table and the table piled with food—herring, lox, bagels, sliced tomatoes, noodle pudding, sour cream. Soon the apartment was jammed with relatives.

Joe and Jack were sitting with some of the uncles, talking serious, grown-up talk. I sat with Heshie and a few of my cousins. They asked if we wanted to go out and play in the street, but that didn't seem right. Besides, we were wearing our good clothes—Heshie his knickers and a white shirt, I, a green dress with green woolen stockings and black shoes with laces.

What was Mama thinking? I glanced at her once in a while as she sat on the maroon couch in front of a window that overlooked a little courtyard. She looked exhausted. Relatives would go over to her, some draping an arm around her and whispering. Occasionally somebody would burst into uncontrollable tears and then it was she who would provide the comforting.

Around me the relatives were talking about the war. German submarines had started sinking American ships and, two weeks ago, President Wilson had declared war on Germany. Even in those two weeks, life around Steelton had changed because of it. In downtown Harrisburg you could see men on street corners shouting about the need to buy Liberty Bonds. On one corner an enormous billboard had gone up with a message that read: FOOD WILL WIN THE WAR, meaning we should eat smaller portions so that we could feed the troops.

Here, at Bubba's, the news from Russia seemed just as important as any word coming from President "Veelson." In one corner of the room two more of Papa's brothers, Uncle Meyer and Uncle Sam, were arguing about some people called Mensheviks and some others called Bolsheviks, and whether a man named Trotsky would be friendlier to the Jews since he was one himself. In another, two cousins whose faces were familiar were talking about whether the revolutionaries had killed the czar and his family or whether they had made the mistake of letting the family survive.

"So you'll move back up here?" my cousin Ruthie asked at one point.

My heart jumped. I looked to Heshie for an answer, but he looked away. This was my problem. "Don't know."

"I mean, will you open the store? Or maybe come back here?"

"Nobody's thinking about it," I said.

"Sure they are," said Ruthie, who read Jane Austen and thought of herself as a sensible girl.

"Like who?"

"Everybody. Uncle Max and Uncle Meyer and Bubba and . . . everybody. And me."

"Oh. I mean, we're not talking about it."

"Think about it now. Everybody here's saying you'll come back."

"We might," Heshie said.

"It'd be great," Ruthie said. "Then we could play together again."

"That would be great," I said.

And then I had to get up and walk over to the dining-room table, pretending I wanted yet another bagel, so Ruthie wouldn't see my eyes well up, because if it came to a choice I would rather we stayed put in Steelton, even if it meant I never played with her again.

I took half a bagel and spread it with whitefish. Turning, I saw that Mama was no longer surrounded by grown-ups; for that moment she was sitting alone. I put down the bagel and walked toward her.

She smiled, put her arms around me, and pulled me onto her lap. I was too old and too big to do that, but I didn't want to hurt her feelings, and actually it was a comfort, feeling softness and warmth through her shiny black dress.

"How's my big girl?" she said in Yiddish.

"Fine."

"A sad day."

"Ruthie wanted us to play outside, but I didn't even want to," I said to show her how affected I had been.

"You can play outside if you want."

"No. I don't want to. Mama?"

"What, *mein kind*?"

"Are we going to move back up here?"

"I don't know."

"Ruthie asked."

"It's something we have to think over," she said. Some of the warmth had gone out of her voice, maybe because she could tell how much I cared—or maybe because it reminded her that there was something we kids wanted that she couldn't provide.

"Which would you like?"

"Ach, I don't know. You want to stay in Steelton."

"Yes."

"I can tell."

The next thing she should have said was *and we will*. There was an awkward silence, until I realized she wasn't going to say it. I slid off her lap. "I'm going to play with Ruthie." What I meant was, if she was thinking about moving back to New York, well, then I would play with Ruthie, sad day or no sad day.

She reached out and stroked my neck to show me that was fine. "Go play," she said, thus showing me it wasn't fine at all.

By nine, the visitors had gone. Bubba was in the kitchen drying what few plates her sisters and cousins hadn't washed for her. Only Mama, the boys, and I, and Mama's sister, Esther, remained. Mama and Esther were talking about Rose and Gert, wondering whether we should have brought them up to New York, too. At one point Mama turned to us and said, "Time for you to go to bed."

The boys headed downstairs: They would stay at Aunt Annie's across the street, all three of them in Annie's double bed, while she would move to the couch.

"What about me?" I asked.

"Oh, for you they got a good place," said Aunt Esther, who lived about five blocks away. She was smiling the way you would if you were giving somebody a present.

Aunt Esther was a large woman—we sometimes called her Aunt Elephant—three years older than Mama. Esther had been married once in Russia. None of us kids knew what had happened except that it was sad and we weren't supposed to ask her about it. She lived alone now, working in a dress factory, which she hated. Because she had no kids, she was the one who had taken care of my other grandma, Mama's mother, when she died. But these days she was as friendly with the Frieds as anyone and was over at Bubba's practically every afternoon.

Aunt Elephant loved us. When she saw us she would throw open her arms. "Birdie! *Mein chachomele!*" she would say—my little genius. And she would embrace us to her enormous bosom, something we endured because it usually came with a dime or even a quarter, which we could spend however we wanted.

"What kind of good place?" I asked her now.

"You'll see."

"It's the couch. I know it's the couch."

She jumped up and led me and Mama down the hall into the bathroom. There was a thick green board slid in between the toilet and the wall. She pulled it out, edging carefully around and setting it down on top of the tub.

"*On* the tub?" I said.

29

"On the tub. That's Bubba's idea."

"But—"

She held up a hand. "Don't worry, this will be comfortable. Believe me. A bed of your own."

"But what if people have to use the bathroom?"

"They'll hold it in," Mama said.

They laughed, but I didn't let myself. I watched while they finished putting down a quilt and a sheet and brought in a couch pillow to put under my head.

"There. How's that?"

"*Very* comfortable," Mama said, flashing me a look that said I should at least sound grateful.

"It's okay."

But once I was in bed, with the lights out, there was no way I could sleep.

This was the bathroom where if you had the lights off for more than ten minutes, roaches congregated in the middle of the floor the way people congregated on Rivington Street in the afternoon! My eyes didn't even feel like closing. I imagined the roaches right beneath me, crawling out from under the tub, waiting right where my feet would land if I got up.

I could hear Mama and Aunt Esther talking in Yiddish down the hall. Their voices were mostly too soft for me to hear what they were saying, but occasionally a word would come through. At one point Esther's voice got loud and I could tell she had moved into the kitchen for something. He was a good husband, she was telling Mama.

I lay still. I was sure roaches wouldn't crawl up the side of the tub, so I felt safe as long as I stayed there. I closed my eyes and after a long while began to relax.

Why did Esther say that? Of course Papa had been a good husband. But hearing that set me thinking. During the last two days, we had been so busy it had been easier to avoid thinking at all. But now I could remember the coughing. I remembered the principal calling me out of class to tell me Papa was in the hospital and I was to go home immediately. I remembered Mama laughing when we kept asking to visit him (*"mein kind*, you'll see him when he gets better"). I remembered the phone ringing one awful night and, a little later, Uncle Izzie pulling up in his car to sweep Mama off to the hospital. And the older kids staying up all night in the house. And then, a few hours later, the phone ringing again, Joe answering, then breaking the news to us, gruffly with the boys, gently with the girls.

How could death happen to a father who would let me count the change each night when he came in from the wagon and who would come around to each bed and say good-night with a little nickname for each of us? Suddenly my throat swelled shut.

"I could come down for a month or so," Esther was saying, still in the kitchen. "Help out with the children."

I couldn't make out Mama's words, but the tone made it clear she was saying it wasn't necessary. Then both voices sank to a murmur again. After a while I heard a door opening and closing, then Mama's heavy tread down the hall toward me. I closed my eyes and pretended to sleep. The door squeaked open. I heard the rustle of a dress next to me and smelled Mama's sour, sweaty smell. I felt the warmth of skin and lips on my forehead.

Should I open my eyes? But by now she might think I had been tricking her. I kept them shut, not daring to move, until I heard her retreat, heard the door close, then heard her steps again, faintly, as she padded down the hall.

Did I have to do that? But it was too late to call out. I lay there for a while, until there was no movement from her. I still couldn't sleep. After what must have been an hour, slowly, half afraid I might crash through the board, I sat, then stood up, reaching for the string to the overhead bulb. I pulled it, watching with a thrill of revulsion as the roaches shot toward holes in the wall or the space underneath the tub.

Maybe I could sleep with the light on.

But that was hopeless, too. By now I couldn't even close my eyes. I got out of bed and walked with my pillow into the dark hallway, past Bubba's room—she was snoring lightly—to the living room. I could see Mama's bulky shape under blankets. Whatever had made me angry with her faded away, and there was nothing more I wanted than to crawl in and snuggle up against her.

There was no room, though. I stood there for a second, thinking about waking her up. Then I sat in the big easy chair nearby, spread the blanket over my curled-up knees, and fell asleep.

When I woke it was morning. Mama was sitting at the kitchen table, wearing her black dress again. Jack and Joe were sitting with her, talking in low voices. Also at the table, with his back to me, but recognizable by his bald spot, was Uncle Max.

Why wasn't he at work? I stood up, stiff from the easy chair, and walked over. The ruins of breakfast filled the plates: half-eaten bagels, drinking glasses with an inch or two of tea, bowls with curds of whitefish and egg salad. The four of them looked over at me as if they wished I were still asleep, but I sat down in the empty chair. "Birdie, you not like your bedroom?" Max asked in English.

"I couldn't sleep."

Mama slapped the table with her palm. "*Oy*, was I surprised. I get out of bed, I look up, and there she is. I thought maybe it was a burglar."

Everybody laughed, too hard. Then the laughter died away and they just sat there, not saying anything. I could tell they had been talking about something serious. They probably didn't want to go back to it while I was around.

Well, tough. I crossed my legs on the chair and tucked my nightgown under my knees so that nobody could see anything.

"So, where do you want to live, little Birdie?" Max said finally.

"I like Pennsylvania," I said in a small voice.

Mama turned to me. "Max says, come back to New York and take a job in the mill."

"Oh."

The boys looked glum. Only Max looked cheerful. "I don't got nothing now," he said. "But in a couple months, we got some big orders. *Then* do we got openings. Boy. Oh, you'll like it, Rivka. Just like a big family party there. Every mornink I come in and there's Meyer, and Irving and Nathaniel and who knows what else? People say if they're not a relative I don't hire them. Look, Rivka, you want your sister to work there, I give her a job, too. Put you right next to each other."

"Max, you're a good person," Mama said in Yiddish.

"Well, I loved Louie," he said. He stood up, cuffing Jack on the head, then looked meaningfully at her. "And you, too."

When he was gone, we sat around the table silently. I reached over for the whitefish.

"So, Mama. What do you think?" Joe asked.

"About what?"

"Working for Uncle Max. That's what you want to do?"

She looked sadly at him. "It's not what I want to do."

"Good."

"It may be what we have to do."

Four

Three days later we returned to Steelton. It was late in the afternoon. We picked up Rose and Gert from Izzie, who said he would be over later, and went home.

It was *erev Shabbes*—Friday night. Usually we would be in synagogue; tonight, Mama said, it was simply too complicated for the family to go. She let the boys go take naps in their rooms or on the couch in the living room, then went to the kitchen. After sundown we weren't allowed to start a fire; it was considered a violation of the sabbath. What we had taken to doing was light the stove in the afternoons, then keep the flame on until Saturday night, the soup simmering the whole time.

In New York we had only iceboxes, large oak cabinets kept cold by big blocks of ice bought from the iceman who would come by every other day. One of the wonders of moving to Harrisburg was that we had a refrigerator there, and we had one in the new house, too. Mama had a big pot of chicken soup stock in it. She took out the pot, put it on the stove, found a few carrots, and reached into a drawer for a knife.

I decided that if she asked me to help, I wouldn't object. She seemed so tired that even I couldn't be angry with her. Besides, although I wouldn't have admitted it, I liked making soup. I liked the act of cutting carrots: cutting off the grimy outside to lay bare the clean, bright orange centers, then chopping them into perfectly even thirds. I liked taking a big pot of broth and gradually filling it with chunks of food that would eventually make everybody's mouth water with its combination of taste and fragrance.

I went into the kitchen and sat at the table. Mama didn't say anything. She began slicing the carrots herself, then, when she was done, pulling apart the chicken left over from the trip home and throwing that into the pot.

She wasn't going to ask me! I sat for a while, watching in disbelief. Mama took a rag from the rag bucket under the sink, wet it, and began wiping up the counter.

"Smells good," I said.

"Yes, it does."

She didn't sound angry. When the counter was dry, she lifted a battered aluminum pot—I remembered Papa bringing it home one evening after one of his trips to the country—and filled it with water for tea.

I thought I was going to cry. I choked it off, though. If she was going to be like that, why volunteer for anything? After a while I went back into the living room, where Heshie was asleep, found *Anne of Green Gables*, which I had read three times, and plunked down into an easy chair with it, hoping Mama would come after me. But the only sounds in the house were the bubbling of the soup and her settling into a kitchen chair, waiting to make her tea.

"Ah, *Shabbes*," Papa would say when he came through the door, as if it were a person waiting to greet him. He loved Friday nights: the glow of candles and the white tablecloth; the way you could walk through the rooms and see everything put neatly away, even our few toys; the way the whole family would gather around the table and wait for him before Mama lit the candles and, hands placed over her eyes, recite the first of the Sabbath prayers.

I think all of us were remembering these things at dinner. It would account for our being so quiet. We gobbled down our food. Jack made a few attempts to start conversation ("Two more days and school again. Right, Heshie?"). But nobody said any more than a few words in answer.

Just as we finished, we heard a car pull up outside. A door slammed. Feet stamped on the wooden porch. Then there was a knock.

"Uncle Izzie," Jack said.

And when we opened the door, he stood in the entrance, taking his cap off and slapping it against his hip a few times before stepping inside to shake off the dust.

There was a good-looking man! Big square jaw. Hair parted in the middle. No beard *or* mustache. Uncle Izzie was actually the first of the uncles to come to Harrisburg. He had a Reo, a big car you could hear from blocks away.

Izzie belonged to the Reform temple, which meant that when he prayed he didn't even wear a skullcap. His store stayed open on Saturday; he allowed only English in his house, and instead of talking to us about the Bible, he liked to tell us how well he and Uncle Raphael were doing, and give us lectures about how wonderful it was to be in America. "You can do anything, here," he would tell us, running a hand through his hair or fingering the gold watch he wore on a chain and would slide into a vest pocket of his suit. "This is America."

He came in, putting up his fists like Jack Dempsey,

knuckles pointed outward, then cuffed the boys on the shoulders, hugged Rose and me, and kissed Mama, saying little teasing things to all of us, even Gert. He made some joke about New York—he had lived there for six months when he came over from Russia and hated it even more than we did. Then he took one of the kitchen chairs, turned it around, and sat so he was straddling it, his chin resting on the back.

"Rivka, we're all sorry," he said in Yiddish. And I remember his voice, full of purpose, the purposefulness of somebody who has to get everyone else to face facts. "It's a shame. But now you got to move on. And here's my question. How're you going to make a living? What about this grocery?"

Gert was chewing on a piece of chicken, looking down at her bowl. The rest of us stopped eating. We practically stopped breathing.

"You call this a grocery?" Mama said. She tossed her head in the direction of the front.

Later—years later—Mama told me she'd been expecting Izzie to show some interest in us. Wasn't it partly his idea that we come down in the first place? But she'd thought if she had said she was going back to New York, he wouldn't argue. He might even have been a little relieved.

But Uncle Izzie was already waving her off. "Because I tell you what. My idea is, open it. I know, I know. From a store you don't know nothing. But this is a good *location*." He leaned over to her, whispering as if he were afraid to let the competition know, *"You can make money here. Believe me."*

"*You* could make money. Me, I'm not so sure."

"We'll show you. I'll show you what to order. I'll

send you my men, they'll show you how to stock shelves, how to keep books. Everything. You got kids here, they can help out. Look, this is America."

"The kids is in school." Mama said in English. It was kind of a rebuke. I think listening to him tell her how much she didn't know, she was a little insulted that he didn't think she could even handle the language. It sounded strange coming out of her mouth.

He switched to English, too. "After school. Before school. There's time. The boys do the heavy work. The girls sveep. Everybody pitch in."

This wasn't just going through the motions. He was urging it on her! Mama looked at Joe. "Yussel, you think is good idea?"

"I think we could do it," Joe said.

"But vat if ve don't do it? Izzie, ve already owe you money."

"Forget the money. We got plenty money."

"I can keep books," Joe said.

I said, "Why don't we get Aunt Esther to come down and help?"

She gave me a look. "You heard her say that?"

"Yes."

"Ven ve vas talking?"

"Yes."

She smiled to show me she wasn't angry. "Vhere vould she sleep?"

"She could sleep with me," I said.

Everybody laughed except Izzie, who didn't know her. He just looked puzzled.

"She would take up the whole bed," Heshie said.

"Maybe two beds," Joe said.

Mama looked annoyed. It was one thing for her to

make fun of her sister, but she didn't like it when we did. "She maybe do that," she said, sounding optimistic for the first time.

I looked around the room. Joe was playing with a spoon. Jack was poking a fat piece of carrot lying in his bowl.

"We'd all work in the store," Jack said.

"There you go," Izzie said.

"I don't vant the boys to vork all the time in the store. I vant they have a profession."

"I agree with you. Tell you what I do. I give Joe a job in my store, assistant to the bookkeeper. If he goes to accounting school, he knows what they're teaching before they teach it. Also, he knows how a store works, he can show you what he learns."

Later, Joe explained how generous Izzie was being: offering to pay him for work Izzie probably didn't really need, helping us set up a store that a few years later might be a rival, even if a relative did own it. Of course, maybe he was so confident, he wasn't afraid of a rival. But Mama was impressed.

"All this to keep us in town?"

He ducked his head. "Whose idea was it you come down here? Besides, Bessie says we can't send you back to New York. That would be mean."

Mama looked at him to make sure he knew she wasn't fooled. "You're very generous, Izzie."

"Well, I got more money, teng God, knock on vood." He rapped the oak table. "And also, I give you vun more reason."

"Vat?"

"Louie. Vat he vould vant you do?"

I was sure that would convince her. But she surprised

40

me. She sat for a few moments. "This I'll have to tink about."

I could see Izzie was exasperated. "Look, Rivka—"

She held up her hand. "Izzie, I mean it. Let me tink."

After he was gone, we sat around the table for a while, as it sank in that for the first time in a week we had nothing to do. Usually, at this hour on a Friday we would be back from shul. Mama and Papa would be putting us to bed, one by one, starting with Gert and Rose. Papa was always happy after services. He would take off his jacket and tie and unbutton the top button on his shirt, and walk around humming tunes from the service. Then he would sit down on the beds to say good-night to each one of us in turn.

For the whole week there had been so much to do— arranging for the body, buying tickets, packing food— that we hadn't had time to realize how much Papa was part of our lives. Now the house seemed full of him.

I remembered something. I went to the front where my pocketbook still sat on the floor, took out the postcard Aunt Yettie had given me, and went back into the kitchen.

"Can I put this in a frame?" I asked.

Mama took it from me. The older boys hadn't seen it yet. Neither had Gert and Rose. They all crowded around to look.

"Papa as a boy," Mama said to Rose. Then, to me: "Would you mind if we put it here?"

"It's mine," I said, then was instantly ashamed.

"Oh, I know. Maybe we could share it, though."

"Sure."

She looked up, and at Joe, her oldest, then set the picture on the table behind her, leaning it against the wall.

"He always wanted to make his mark on the world. And what's left? A few pictures."

"Six children," Jack said, a little reproachfully.

"Six wonderful children, yes. But he had such plans! He didn't even get to open this store."

"*Aruf arbeten,*" Joe said.

It was such a perfect imitation we all had to laugh. Then nobody spoke. I could hear a horse clop-clopping outside in the street.

"He deserved more," Mama said. And then she turned to Joe. "You think Izzie, he's right? With his help we could do this?"

"Yes," Joe whispered. It was the way people who climb mountains whisper, afraid of starting an avalanche.

"And everybody wants to stay here?"

We all nodded, or else murmured, "Yes, yes, Mama."

"This will be hard."

"We know that, Mama," Jack said.

"Okay," she said, in English, trying, and failing, to sound American. "Ve do it!"

Five

Was there some sort of catch? But then Jack and Joe let out whoops. Heshie was grinning, and when he saw Gert and Rose looking confused, he leaned across the table. "We're not going back to smelly New York," he said.

I realized Mama meant what she'd said. Had I misjudged her entirely? "Oh, thank you, Mama," I said. She was smiling and looking at us as if to say, "Didn't I come through?" Then everybody burst into questions. Joe went down to the cellar and brought up a bottle of wine, and for the rest of the evening the boys sat around talking about things that could make customers come to the store while the other girls played and I listened, until it was time to get up and go to our beds.

Waking up the next morning I was scared again. Something could still go wrong. But on Monday evening Mama, Joe, and I went into Harrisburg to Izzie's store. He wanted to show us things he felt he couldn't describe.

We arrived after he had closed up. The front door was locked. Passersby were looking in curiously to see why the place was still lit up. We were special! We had a privilege others didn't—an in with someone who was definitely on his way up! How could we possibly fail, especially when we looked at what he had built—as he told us several times—"from notink"?

Uncle Izzie's long, narrow rectangle of a store had three times the space that we had. It was lined on both sides with glass cases and shelves. On the shelves were dried goods and canned goods. In back were the freezer locker and a refrigerated glass case—"The latest," Izzie said—displaying meats. On the back wall was a display of pots and pans and muffin tins and molds, and above that a sign that read WELCOME! IF WE PLEASE YOU, TELL OTHERS. IF WE DON'T PLEASE YOU, TELL US!

He led us to the front, where there were not one, but two, cash registers, ornate brass ones with borders of oak trim, set atop a long counter. In front of the counter were barrels of pickles and cornflakes, and behind glass and in glass jars were candies—licorice drops and taffy, and the things we called dots, long strips of paper with different-colored hard round candies stuck to them. "You keep these in front. Lots of people, they pull out their money, and here's the little one, like Rose, she says, 'Please, give me some dots.' And they do. The glass, everything looks shiny. The price is right. Everything very colorful. Maybe a penny, they buy. Maybe two pennies."

He was talking very fast. The only trouble was, he was saying everything to Joe, in English, as if Mama were just along for the ride.

"Vun penny, two pennies. It adds up," Mama said in English, trying to be part of the conversation.

"That's right. That's right. It's like the old joke! The man had a store, made a *lot* of money, a *lot*. And somebody asks him, they ask, 'How you do so well?' He says, 'Dunt be too greedy. Buy your candy for vun cent, sell for two cent. Be heppy vid a vun percent profit.' "

He broke into a barking laugh, hitting Joe between the shoulder blades. Mama didn't laugh. Neither did I. "I don't get it," I said.

Joe looked down at me. "One percent, Birdie. He thought a cent was a percent. He was marking up a hundred percent."

Izzie was still laughing. "Rivka, you got a smart boychick."

Mama's face was still a blank. Izzie stopped, looking concerned, as if afraid he had hurt her feelings. But then the beginning of a smile crept over her face. In Yiddish she said, hesitantly, "One hundred percent, that's from one cent to two cents."

"Right. Right."

She began laughing. Izzie began laughing again, relieved. Then Joe laughed, pounding his hand on the corner of the glass candy display case. Finally I did, still not sure I understood, but making sure I was laughing loud enough so everyone could hear.

The next night, Izzie came over to our house, this time with a long list written out by hand on sheets of yellow paper. He sat at the kitchen table, going over it with Mama, Joe, and Jack. What to order. How much of each. Which things sold out fastest. Who the suppliers would be. What we had to order every day and what we could order once a week.

When he was gone, and the dishes were washed and put away in the cabinets, Mama sent us into the living room. She took Joe with her into the kitchen.

She had decided she needed Aunt Esther. Normally, she would have written her a letter—in those days you dialed long distance only in an emergency—but the thought of going even a week without knowing was unbearable. So, after a lot of discussion, and after figuring

45

out exactly how much it would cost for each minute, Mama had decided, well, if this wasn't an emergency, what was?

From the living room I could hear Joe in his soberest voice: "Operator? I would like to place . . ." He must have passed the phone to Mama. There was a long silence. Then, in Yiddish, *"Esther? Du herst?"* Do you hear?

They talked for about five minutes, Mama telling her what she had decided, reminding her of her offer, and asking her to come down. Then Mama was thanking her, and saying that she loved Esther, and wasn't the telephone something, but it cost a lot of money, too, and give a kiss to everybody.

"She's coming?" Heshie said when Mama came back into the living room.

Mama shrugged. "She has to think it over."

"Why?"

"I don't know."

"Maybe she's got a fella," Jack said.

"That's not funny."

"Sorry, Mama."

"Next week she'll call."

"Let's hope so," Mama said.

We spent the next two weeks, every moment we weren't in school, getting ready. We gave the store a final cleaning. We swept the floors. We washed the counters.

The vendors started coming over with order blanks. In those days, when the egg man came with eggs or the pickle man with a barrel of pickles, you didn't write him a check. You usually handed over the money for it right then in greasy dollar bills taken from the register. But Uncle Izzie, who by now was a big account for them, had asked them to supply us on credit. This meant we could wait until the end of the month to pay, after we had some money coming in. So we would order in the quantities Izzie had suggested we use, and each time Mama would look over the order forms, pretending to check what she couldn't really read, and sign her name.

Now trucks from the suppliers began pulling up in front. Workmen would come in with cases of crackers and canned soups, bottles of soda pop and the barrels of cornflakes we had seen in Izzie's store. The boys would unpack the boxes and stock the shelves. They gave me the job of breaking down the boxes. I would take each empty one, pull it apart, then stamp on it till it was flat. Then Jack or Heshie would carry the boxes, three or four at a time, out to the back. When they got a big pile, they would take them down to the dump.

Except for the boxes and some cleaning up, there wasn't much work the boys were going to give a girl. So in the afternoons, when school was out, I had plenty of time to watch, or take walks with Rose.

We wouldn't walk far. In Mama's opinion, it wasn't safe. Just beyond our neighborhood was a long street lined with shacks, really. Some weren't even painted. They had one or two rooms. Water came from pumps outside the cabins. There was no electricity and there were no bathrooms. There were outhouses in back, and if you walked down the street around six-thirty in the evening, you would see men outside each house, stripped to the waist, standing in front of basins of cold water, washing grime off their bodies.

We called these people hunkies, which in those days meant that they came from Hungary. This shabby neighborhood we called Hunkytown. Living there were the men who worked in the steel mills, the huge factories you could see from anywhere in town, sending fire and smoke and great big showers of sparks and ash into the air.

I had an image of what these mills looked like inside: great vats of red, molten metal being stirred by dirty men with greasy hair, an image probably based on something I had seen in a book. But we had never been inside. We didn't know anyone who had, despite the fact that half of my classmates had fathers who worked there. The reason was that, although we talked to the hunky kids at school and waved when we saw them in the street, we played only with Jewish kids, and the Jewish families were the only ones my parents knew. And no Jewish family would even think of working in the mills.

"Why they work in such a place?" Mama would say, looking at the showers of sparks and ash raining from the big brick smokestacks that rose above a mill.

Joe: "They have to make a living."

"Such dirty work."

I agreed with her. I wondered why the hunkies didn't open stores or factories the way the Jews did.

But the question didn't even occur to me when it came to the people living a few blocks farther away, along streets shabbier than Hunkytown. They were the people Mama insisted we call "colored." *The* colored. That was out of respect. One time a friend of Heshie's had said he was going to walk past "Niggertown." Mama didn't know much English, but she knew that word; she ordered him out of the house. "Ve vere slaves in Egypt," she said. "Pipple probably called us names, too."

Sometimes you could see black men in town, working as carpenters' helpers, always for a white carpenter. Or they would drive wagons for the storekeepers. Or help in

people's yards. A lot of the black women worked as maids, and in the mornings, on our way to school, we would see them walking to the other side of town, where the big houses were. But in this neighborhood, most of the men worked at a mill, although doing the worst jobs.

There were some black kids in my class at school, but not many. They were very quiet. They never asked questions. At recess, the three black girls in my class huddled together on the playground, talking so seriously that for a while I thought maybe black kids didn't like to smile.

One day, though, I came around the corner of the school building and saw the group of them laughing, heads thrown back. They saw me and stopped. One of them said, "Hi."

"Hi," I said. We stared at each other for a few seconds. They looked scared, as if I had caught them smoking cigarettes. I turned and went back the way I'd come. When I turned the corner I heard them start talking again.

The teachers didn't like them much, especially Miss Cleary, our teacher, a bony woman who wore her gray hair in a bun and seemed to think personal appearance was the most important thing in the entire world. Miss Cleary would line up her class each morning for inspection. We would have to stand straight, hands at our sides, book bags on the ground. Then, hands behind her back, she would walk slowly around us, making sure that the creases were sharp in the boys' pants and their sleeves were buttoned at the cuff, not rolled up, or that the seams in the wool stockings we girls wore were even and our shoes had been polished until they shone. "Wesley, what's that lump in your pocket? A jackknife? Why, Wesley, you know I don't allow such things in the classroom. Hand it over. Class! Listen to me, class. You boys should have

smooth pockets. Don't need to bring anything to school causes a lump. If I see it, I'll ask for it and I'll confiscate it. Know what that means? Confiscate? Means I'll take it from you, and goodness knows when you get it back. Maybe never. Okay. Into the classroom. March."

Blanche Strasser used to say her stockings made her legs itch, and in fact, if you looked at her legs, they always had red welts running up the calves, which she insisted went away as soon as she went home and changed clothes.

One day in February she had come without them, hoping Miss Cleary wouldn't see. No such luck. "Blanche, your stockings," Miss Cleary said.

"Miss Cleary, they make my legs itch."

"Do you have a note from the doctor to that effect?"

"No."

"Then you have to wear them."

"I left them home."

"Bring them tomorrow."

Miss Cleary had her nice moments. When the white kids asked her questions, she would smile and touch us on the shoulder, and talk about what clever questions we'd asked. But when black kids asked, there was no expression on her face, and she seemed to answer only because she had to.

One of the black girls was Roxanne Johnson, who sat next to me in class. She was quiet, like the others. She had two younger brothers who flanked her when she came walking up to school each morning. You could tell she was poor because she had two dresses, a green cotton dress that she wore most days, and a brown one that looked as if it were made out of a burlap bag. Even I had more dresses than that.

I liked school, though I wouldn't admit it to anybody.

And after a while I noticed that Roxanne did, too. She came every day. Even on days when she was sick, she would come to school, wiping her nose every five minutes with a cotton hanky, but never letting her eyes waver from Miss Cleary, not even to pass a note or look out the window.

At first we didn't talk to each other. In the morning, or after recess, before we lined up to go inside, the black kids were off in one corner, the Jews in another, and the hunkies—that is, most of the kids—were all around.

One week, though, Roxanne was so sick she *did* stay home, and when she returned she came up to me before the morning bell and asked if I could show her the math homework for the week she was out, probably because she knew I kept the old assignments clipped into the back of my notebook, which I had in my hand. "Okay," I said. "But why don't you ask Miss Cleary?"

"Oh," she said. "She don't like me."

Roxanne looked at me as if she dared me to deny it. But how could I? I got out my notebook. "Here it is," I said.

"Sorry about your Dad," said Blanche on Monday as I walked with Heshie onto the playground.

"Yeah, sorry, Birdie," Sophie Weingarten said.

"Sorry," said Toby Klein.

"Thanks," I said. Heshie went off to his friends, and I sat down next to the three girls along the wire fence that ran around the school playground.

"My dad says he was a *haimisher* fellow," Sophie said—a nice guy.

Except she said it wrong. She said *hee*misher. Sophie's parents had both been born in America. She didn't speak Yiddish at all. I didn't correct her, though. She was trying.

"How was New York?" Toby said.

"I didn't see much."

"Dummy. She went for a funeral. Probably you sat *shiva* the whole time."

"Except for the funeral."

"That's sad," Toby said.

"Are you going to move up there?" Sophie asked.

"No. We're going to open the store."

"Yay!"

"Uncle Izzie's going to help us."

"He's rich," said Toby, whose parents shopped in Izzie's store.

"He's not rich," I said. That made it sound like I had an unfair advantage.

"Well-to-do."

"Maybe. His store is big." Then I changed the subject. "What did I miss?" I asked.

"Nothing."

"One thing," Toby said.

"Oh yeah," Sophie said.

"Tell me."

"We're going to start a club. The JGC."

"Know what it is?"

"The Jewish Girls' Club," I said. Sophie had mentioned it to me probably a dozen times that month. Then she had stopped, and because I was new in town it had crossed my mind that she had decided not to include me.

"How'd she know?" Toby asked.

"She's smart," Sophie said.

"Who's going to be in it?" I asked before Toby could say anything.

"Not everybody."

"But I am. That's why you're telling me."

"Of course, silly."

I smiled, as if I had had no doubt about it.

"We meet once a week, each time at another kid's house," Sophie said.

"What do we do?"

"I'm glad you asked," she said. Reaching into her green book bag, she pulled out a notebook and started to open it. But just then the bell rang. All of us jumped to our feet. Miss Cleary was already outside by the door.

Blanche was walking with Toby. I fell in beside Sophie. "You want to sleep over my house?" she asked. "Mama says it's all right."

"Sure. Let me ask my mama, but yeah."

"Great."

We walked along, not saying anything. I'd been at the school three months, but I felt I'd finally made a friend.

Behind us when we got into line were Roxanne and another one of the black girls. "Hi, Roxanne," I said.

"Hi. Sorry 'bout your daddy."

"Thanks," I said.

"You friends with her?" Sophie whispered as soon as we were inside.

I felt a chill run through me, the way I felt if Mama asked me if I'd cleaned the bathroom. "Not friends."

"I don't even talk to them," Sophie said. "They're scary. They never smile. Ever notice that? They never smile."

"They smile," I said. "They're just scared of Cleary."

"Papa says don't even talk to them."

"Just because you say hello doesn't make you a friend," I said, hoping she didn't take offense.

Six

Joe decided to take Uncle Izzie up on his offer. Three days that week he would head into Harrisburg after school, coming back barely in time for dinner. Meanwhile people had seen that the store was opening. A few times each day, someone would come up the steps, knock on the door, and come in looking to buy something. Some of them couldn't read Jack's OPEN SOON sign. Some of them could, but figured that since we had things on the shelves, why not sell to them?

"Vell, vy not?" Mama said when, two days before the official opening, one of the hunkies came in asking for a pound of salami, sixteen cents a pound. She took a salami out of the glassed-in case, whacked off a piece, put it delicately on the scale, then went over to the cash register Uncle Izzie had lent to us.

I remember her pressing the cash register buttons a little gingerly, as if they might explode. "Vun . . . six . . ."

The register drawer sprang open. A smile appeared on her face. She had done it right. "And here your change."

There was a big discussion one night about whether or not to give credit—that is, to allow customers to charge purchases, running up a bill until the end of the month, when they could pay it all. It was basically what we were doing with our own suppliers. But Uncle Izzie told us that under no circumstances should we give credit for the first three months at least, and then only sparingly.

"But you do it," Joe had told him.

He laughed. "Very good, Joe. That's very good. For people they been my customers a year. Two years. I know them. I know where they work. These are people who got money in the bank. Otherwise, no."

That sounded good to Mama. No credit, she decided. Jack and Joe nodded soberly to make it clear they agreed.

Mama decided to keep the store open six days a week. "Also at night," she said. In those days, when a lot of houses didn't have electricity, people shopped in the daytime. But even if we took in another two or three dollars each evening, it would help. We would keep the light on in the store all evening, and one of us would take turns sitting in there for any families who wanted to come by.

One night Mama announced that she wanted to start speaking English around the house. "For customers is good I speak," she said at dinner. "All you kids, you talk in English to me. Ven I learn, den dey understand me more better."

And here was another question only she could decide. Would we sell ham? It wasn't kosher, of course, and even the thought of handling it seemed repulsive. But when she brought it up to Uncle Izzie on one of the nights he was eating with us, he surprised us by almost insisting on it. It was the most popular meat with the Christians, he said.

Mama listened to him and thought a moment. "No," she said.

"Rivka. It's selling only. Not eating."

"Izzie, I can't."

"*Touching. Touching only.* Touching isn't chewing."

"No, no, no," she said, sounding embarrassed, as if afraid he might think her unforgivably naive.

He looked at her for a second, and I thought he would argue some more. But he just threw up his hands. "Okay, okay. On that you make up your own mind."

And she was firm about another thing. We would close the store at sundown Friday, the beginning of *Shabbes.* We wouldn't reopen until Sunday morning.

The boys didn't like that idea. They didn't have the nerve to argue about it, though. All Joe said was, "That's a big shopping day."

"Papa would not want his store open on *Shabbes,*" Mama said. "And this is—was—his store."

"Okay, okay. Whatever you say, Ma."

So on Friday, precisely at sundown, one week and two days before we opened, the work we were doing on the store stopped. Mama and I had spent the afternoon scrubbing the rest of the house—I didn't help in the kitchen anymore, but I still cleaned. We set the dining-room table. Mama lit the candles. Without rolling his eyes, Joe said the *hamotzie,* the prayer over bread, and the *broche,* over the wine. And we settled down to a *Shabbes* dinner a lot like the ones we had always had— except without Papa.

Sunday night, when Gert and Rose were asleep and I was already in my nightgown, the phone rang. Jack answered. "Mama, it's Aunt Esther," he said.

I could hear her drop something with a clatter and head for the kitchen. I got out of bed and followed her. Jack and Joe were sitting by the table, watching her. Heshie was leaning against the wall.

56

Mama sat, holding the phone to her ear the way she always did, with both hands, as if this mysterious and delicate instrument might explode. She was nodding. When Heshie moved, making the floorboards creak, she whipped around and put a finger to her lips. And then she broke into a broad smile. "Oh, Es. I'm so happy," she said.

Heshie raised his hands in the air as if he were lifting weights. Jack looked at Joe and formed a circle with his thumb and index finger. Joe was smiling and nodding.

"She's coming!" Mama said when she hung up.

The following Sunday she arrived, large as ever, in a long blue dress with a high neck and round white collar, and a steel watch pinned to her chest. She brought three suitcases, lots of hugs, and a bag full of *zemels* for everybody.

Where would she sleep? With Mama, it turned out, in the double bed, right on the spot where Papa had lain. That seemed kind of strange to me but if the others felt that way they didn't mention it.

That night, the night before we officially opened, we sat around the table, Mama, Esther, and the six kids. I sat with Heshie. Mama sat at the head of the table, with Joe on one side and Jack on the other.

"This is what we have to do," Joe said, very aware that he was the oldest. "We have to sell forty dollars a day."

"What happens if we sell less?" Heshie asked.

Joe looked at the figures on the pad in front of him. "If we sell forty dollars, we break even. There's no money for us, but we pay our creditors."

"Less than that?"

"Less than that, we can't even pay them."

"We owe them money," Heshie said.

"That's right. We close the doors."

"And go to jail."

"No. We'd have to pay them back. But they'd give us time."

"We could borrow from Uncle Izzie."

"No," Mama said. "He give us too much already."

But she was excited. She stood up. She began pacing around the room. "Remember. Izzie says don't tink ve get forty dollars today. Not right avay. Dis takes time. Ve try tings dat maybe don't vork. Ve make mistakes. And ve learn. Ve can do dis."

"I know," Heshie said. "This is America." The boys all started laughing. The girls looked up, kind of puzzled, but then they were laughing, too, because all of a sudden everybody seemed happy. Then we went to bed.

Did I sleep at all that night? I don't think so. I remember lying in bed, listening to Jack and Joe moving up and down the stairs while it was still dark outside. They were getting ready for the produce man, who was coming with our vegetables. I heard everything: his truck pulling up, the joking between him and the boys, then the heavy stomping up the wooden stairs, the squeak of the door as they opened it for him to come through.

A little later, the dairyman came. Milk didn't come in cartons then. It came in a big metal barrel that stayed in the front of the store. People would come with their own pitchers. We'd dip into the barrel with a long-handled ladle and fill their pitchers. I heard the dairyman roll the barrel off the truck, then tramp up the steps and set it down in the store.

None of us wanted to go to school. We wanted to stay and watch the customers come in. But Mama wouldn't hear of it.

"We opened our store today," I told my friends during the day. Partly I was telling them the news. But partly I was trying to drum up business. Wouldn't it be wonderful if I did? Wouldn't it be wonderful if the customers who brought in that forty dollars a day came from my friends in school? At the end of recess, I found myself next to Roxanne. I looked around. Sophie wasn't anywhere in sight. "My mama opened our store today," I said, realizing as I said it that I had never started a conversation with her before.

"Oh yeah? What kind?"

"Grocery," I said.

"Oh," she said. She walked on. I thought she was mad about something. But then she looked back at me. "That's nice."

Usually, at the end of school, Heshie waited for me. We would walk together to the back entrance, where the younger kids were let out, and wait for Rose. Then the three of us would walk home together. I liked having Rose along: I could boss her around, telling her to stop at corners or hold my hand crossing. But this time, what a pain! Heshie had run home alone, and I had to crawl because Rose couldn't keep up!

I had visions of the store being crowded, but it was empty except for Heshie and Mama and Aunt Esther, who stood beside the register.

"How much did we sell?" I asked.

"Three dollars, eighty-four cents," Aunt Esther said.

Three eighty-four! Even I knew how little that was. The day was almost over! "But we need forty dollars!"

They laughed. Aunt Esther came over and clasped me to her chest, which was a little like being smothered by an enormous pillow. Her watch pressed into my head. "This is our first day, *mein kind*. Don't worry about it."

Just then, two women from Hunkytown came up the steps. They smiled their gold-toothed smiles at Mama and Aunt Esther. Mama smiled at them. They walked up and down the aisles, talking softly to each other in what I could now recognize was Hungarian.

I didn't move. I couldn't. I pretended I wasn't looking at them. I thought I should open a schoolbook or talk to Mama, but I couldn't think of anything to say.

"I'm going to the bathroom," Heshie said. He disappeared back into the house.

One of the women came to the front. She picked up a wicker basket, then went up the aisles, putting in soup cans. At the vegetable counter, she picked up some bunches of carrots by the green stems, looking them over. Into the basket they went. Then in went celery and some cheese.

The other one got a basket. She came up to Mama and pointed to the coffee machine, then the barrel of coffee beans.

"Vun pound?"

"Ya."

"You vant grind it?"

"Ya."

That was Heshie's job. But he was still gone. Mama scooped out some beans, dumped them in, and started the motor, trying to look as if she did it all the time. The women took out identical black change purses. They counted out bills. Mama rang up first 83¢, then $1.03. "You have children?"

They looked at her, not understanding.

Mama pointed to me. They smiled. "Ya. Ya."

Mama reached into the candy jar inside the show-case. She put two sour balls into the bag.

"Tank you, tank you," one of them said. Everybody laughed.

After they left, Aunt Esther looked at Mama approvingly. "They'll be back," she said.

"Don't expect too much," Uncle Izzie had told us. So when we finished the first day with nine dollars, we tried not to worry. Izzie came over the second night, too, unexpectedly. He was just checking up. Were we learning? Did we like the suppliers?

Mama said yes.

Right in front of us kids, Izzie offered to lend us money for the next month. But Mama waved him off. She thought that we had borrowed enough from him.

I'm not sure why. My guess is that as nice as he was, she still felt you couldn't ask so much from someone who wasn't a blood relative. Anyway, there would be no more borrowing from Uncle Izzie.

On Wednesday, Heshie met me after school with a surprise.

"Birdie, look at this," he said.

I looked. He was holding a sheet of paper by one corner between his thumb and index finger. I remember thinking how black the rims of his nails were. GRAND OPENING! GROCERY STORE! the paper read. NEW IN NEIGHBORHOOD! In smaller type it had our address and the hours.

"Where'd you get this, Hesh?"

"Print shop at school. Did it myself. Look, I got five hundred of them."

He motioned with his head to a folder strapped in

with his books. "See, nobody knows we're open. I'm going to put one on every house in the neighborhood. Want to help?"

"Sure."

We took Rose home. Then, that afternoon, we spent three hours going up and down the streets.

It was May, but the day was cool. We walked into the wind. At first, even though he had asked me to come, Heshie didn't seem to trust me. *He* carried the pack of fliers. He would give me one and point to a house, as if deciding which houses got the fliers, which was silly since we were doing every house. But never mind. I would run up and put it on the porch, or if the house had a screen door, between the door and door frame. If people happened to be on the porch, I would thrust it at them until someone extended a hand. Then I hurried back for the next one.

Soon Heshie saw it would be faster if I just worked one side of the street while he worked the other, and that's what we did.

It was late afternoon. None of the men were around—they were all at the mill. Kids were home from school. A lot of mothers were out on the front porches, playing with babies or yelling to the older kids in Hungarian. Once in awhile I saw somebody from my school and we would nod.

At one point, we came to the end of Hunkytown and looked across to the first of the streets where the "coloreds" lived.

"Do we go down there?"

For the first time, I saw Heshie uncertain. "I don't know," he said.

"Is it safe?"

"It's safe. I just don't know if Mama—"

"If Mama what?"

"None of your business. Let's go home."

I knew what was bothering him. Should we give fliers to the black families? Talking about them with respect was one thing. Going up and down their streets and asking them to come into our store was something else.

I was uncomfortable going along with him, but I wasn't sure what I didn't like, or even how to bring it up. I knew one thing: I wasn't going to argue about it; Heshie might not want to take me next time if I did. And when we got back home I stopped caring, because we saw there were actually people walking down the street toward the store, some of them holding the fliers we had handed them not an hour before!

We just about flew up the steps and through the screen door. For the first time since the store had opened, there were more than four people inside, all women.

My heart started to pound! Heshie and I looked at each other, smiling.

But as we came up to the counter, I saw Mama talking to one of the women. She looked worried. The woman was holding up little slips of blue paper. The woman said, "You use?"

"No," Mama said. "Ve cannot use."

Seven

It wasn't until dinnertime that I got an explanation I could understand. It came from Joe, who by this time had spent a few afternoons in Izzie's store and knew some things the rest of us didn't.

The steel mills didn't pay most of their workers in cash, Joe told us. Instead they gave out little pieces of blue paper that up close looked like play money, with values printed in the corners and an oval picture in the center, not of George Washington, but of a man with a small pointy beard and round spectacles named Samuel F. Waters, President of the Great Northeastern Steel Company. The paper was called scrip.

Joe said, "Great Northeastern, they're no different than any other mill. They all of them have stores that sell groceries, clothes, everything you want. The prices are high, and they take the scrip. The mills make money that way. Lots of money. These people would like to buy from us, but first they gotta get someone to pay them for their scrip. In dollars."

"Which some people do," Jack said.

"Yeah."

"Vat you mean?" Mama asked.

"Say you have a dollar's worth of scrip," Jack said. He was showing us he knew something, too. "Some people will buy it for ninety cents. You lose some value on it, but then you have money. Real money. Money you can use anywhere."

"Course, most workers are afraid to do that. Anyway, that's what Uncle Izzie says," Joe said.

"Vy?"

"Well, because the mill doesn't like it. Figure it out. If these people go to us, they don't buy at the Northeastern store. This makes the owners mad. They might even fire people if they find out."

The point was, a lot of the families had seen our flier and wanted to shop with us. But only the ones willing to take the risk of trading in their scrip for cash could do it. And there was another problem. A surprising number of people had asked if we could give them food on credit.

Joe explained that, too. "I guess a lot of these families get paid once a week. Or once every two weeks. I don't know. They'd like us to let them shop each day, keep a list of what they owe us, then they come in at the end of the month and pay up."

Rose asked, "What's bad about that?"

"Well, let's say they can't pay. Or they leave town. Then we're out a lot of money."

"Aren't watchamacallits, the suppliers, giving *us* credit?" I asked.

"Because Uncle Izzie asked them to. If we skip town, they go to him. They know he'll cover us."

"Yeah, we can't do that. Uncle Izzie said we'd be crazy if we did that," Joe said. He looked at Mama, smiling, as if it were kind of charming that little Rose could be so ignorant.

To my surprise, Mama didn't look certain at all. "Vell, I don't know. Dese vimmin look like gut pipple."

"Oh, Mama," Joe said. "You can't tell by looks."

"Izzie said what? Wait three months, right?" Heshie asked.

"Three months and then only to people who proved themselves," Jack said.

"I guess dat's right. Ve say no."

I could see relief in the way Joe leaned back in his chair.

"A lot of people gonna be disappointed. Maybe I should stop giving out any more fliers, all those problems."

"Oh, no, Heshie. Dese fliers of yours. Dat vus very good."

"I helped," I said, feeling slighted.

"You did. Oh, you certainly did."

We were studying averages in school, and it was a good thing because that first week it was all Joe and Jack talked about. We took in $9 a day Monday and Tuesday, in those days when bread was a nickel a loaf. But on Wednesday, the day we distributed the fliers, we did $12, Thursday, $14. Friday was light—$8. We were closed on Saturday, of course, but on Sunday we did $18. And during the next week we watched our sales inch up each day. $21. $23. $25. On Friday they were back down to $16, for reasons we couldn't understand. Then, the next Sunday, $25 again.

"Is better. But not enough," Mama said.

She had become very enthusiastic about speaking English. As each customer came in and she saw she knew the words for what she wanted to say, she would find excuses to say things to them—the kind of friendly, non-essential chatter she imagined might keep them coming back.

One afternoon that week, I was sitting behind the counter, doing homework, when two women came up to the cash register, counting out change for bread and roast beef. With them was a little girl named Anna I had seen walking into the second-grade classroom at school. Mama noticed her looking down into the pickle barrel, where the pickles floating in the dark brine looked like the bellies of green whales. "You vunna peekl?" Mama asked.

Maybe if she had gestured with her hands it would have been clear. But she was busy running up totals. "Guhead. Tek," she said.

The women looked at each other, then at Mama. They smiled. "Good day to you," one of them said, in a different accent, but one almost as thick.

After they were gone I mustered up my courage and said, "Mama, they didn't understand you."

"I know. De hunkies, dey don't speak English."

"Not the way you said it."

"I deedn't say gut?"

I shook my head.

"Mama," Heshie said, "it's *pik-il*. Not *peekl*."

"Peek-el," Mama said.

"Pickle. Pih. Pih."

"Pih. Pihkle."

"That's good."

"Vat elze?"

Heshie and I looked at each other. We weren't comfortable with the idea of teaching her something.

"Well," I said, "don't say *vun*. It's *one*. One."

"Wuh," Heshie said. "Double-u."

67

"Wwwuh," she said, looking as if she had to force her lips to move, the way you do when you've been out in the cold for a long time.

"That's it," I said.

"Your own children teaching you to speak," Esther said in Yiddish, sounding amused.

"Tings you know ven you ver tree," Mama said.

"*When* you were three," I said.

For a second she looked annoyed. But then she remembered she had asked for it. "Wwwhen. When. When."

Sophie's front lawn rose up from the street, split by two flights of cement steps that led to a screened-in front porch. I could hear music as I came up the steps, and when I came through the front door Mrs. Weingarten was sitting at the piano. At first I thought she was playing, but when she turned around the music kept going and I saw she was pumping a pedal with both feet.

"A player piano," I said. "I love them."

It was Thursday of the third week we were open. After a lot of discussion Mama had decided I could sleep over at Sophie's house even though it was a weekday, and now, as I came inside, I hoped I would feel comfortable. The place looked so sophisticated. The living-room floor was covered with a rug that had two peacocks woven into a design, and around the room were all kinds of things—a Victrola on an oak stand, a stereopticon with some slides scattered around, Chinese-looking vases with paper flowers—things I had seen only in the Sears catalogue.

Sophie smiled. "You can play music from those rolls—that's 'Alexander's Ragtime Band' by Irving Berlin, who's Jewish, you know. But also—Mom, show her—you can play it like a real piano."

Her mother was smiling. She turned a key. The music stopped. "I'll play what I've been practicing," she said, sounding eager to perform. Then she swiveled her chair around and played a little of a piece I'd heard in school.

"Chopin," Sophie said.

How could I possibly feel comfortable in such a house?

But I had a good time. We walked around the neighborhood. I looked at Sophie's collection of dolls—she was too old for them now, she told me. We went up to her room and played cards with her two sisters. And after dinner we all sat around the piano singing songs until it was time to go upstairs, where her mother had made up the second bed in Sophie's room and turned down the covers.

"Did you like doing this?" Sophie asked in the morning when, book bags over our backs, we were walking down the long streets between her house and the school.

"I've never seen a house so nice. Except my uncle's. Maybe his."

"Oh, Isadore. My papa knows him," she said.

For some reason that annoyed me. I was afraid she was telling me that while we were Izzie's poor relations, they were his friends. Anyway, I was tempted to invite her to sleep over at my house. Where would we put her, though? On the couch? That seemed good enough for the relatives—actually, I'd fallen asleep on it myself, and it was pretty comfortable. But it was shabby compared to what Sophie's parents had given me.

Still, hadn't we learned in school that differences in the money people had didn't matter, that all were equal in the sight of God? And hadn't we just had a friendly night together? "I'd like to have you over. If you don't mind sleeping on the couch."

"God, the couch," she said. "I don't know if I'm up to that." She was smiling. But I could tell it was the last thing she would ever want to do.

We were getting to know the suppliers. The ones who came before three o'clock I never saw, naturally. But there were some who came at the end of the day, pulling up in their trucks—one or two still had horse-drawn wagons—unloading cases of cereal or apples or cheese and bringing them into the store. Most of them were friendly, and there was only one we all disliked: Dorfschneider, the bakery man, a short, squat man with straight blond hair and a walrus mustache, who, along with the Milton bakery, supplied breads and pies.

Uncle Izzie had warned us about him. He said Dorfschneider was honest but unpleasant. About his honesty we couldn't say. He was curt but polite during those first weeks. But Monday of the fourth week we were open, he came stomping up the steps with a load of cakes and breads, put the boxes on the floor, then took out the cakes and loaves so we could count them. "Boyoboy, you people are taking over the whole town," he said. He was still panting.

"Vat you mean?"

"Frieds everywhere. You Jewish people, right?"

"Right," said Mama.

"When you get off the boat?"

"I come to Ellis Island vas 1893."

He bent down, came up with a box of little frosted cakes, and dropped it on the counter—too heavily, I

70

thought, as if he wouldn't mind if a few cakes broke. "My people been here almost a hundred years, we don't got stores like you people got."

"Well," Joe said at dinner that night, after we repeated what Dorfschneider had said, "who knows how long we'll have this one?"

Why he picked that moment to become so garrulous, I don't know. But while I didn't exactly understand what was so bad about what Dorfschneider had said, Mama and the older boys seemed very offended. After dinner, though, Heshie and Joe disappeared into the store, and soon Joe stood in the hallway, smiling, clearly somebody with a trick up his sleeve. "Okay, everybody, close your eyes," he said.

"Close your eyes. Close your eyes," Gert said.

I did, at any rate. I could hear the rip of cardboard and the clank and scrape of knives on plates.

"Okay, open," Joe said.

I opened my eyes. On each of our plates were two thin slices of apple pie.

"One of these is Milton. The other, Dorfschneider," Joe said. "Which is which?"

"And which is better?" Heshie said.

"Right, right. Which is better?"

You could tell which was which right away. The Milton pies were so much thinner, just the way they looked in the box. But we took our bites, anyway. And when it came to taste, the difference was just as clear. The Milton pie was soggy: the filling was more like applesauce, although I still liked it. Dorfschneider's apple pieces were big and sweet, with dark juice, and cinnamon specks floating in the juice, and the crust was flaky.

"He may be a scoundrel, but he knows how to bake," Jack said.

Three days later, Dorfschneider came in to make his next delivery. It was late in the afternoon. I was sitting at a table near the cash register, doing homework. "You bake a veddy nize pie, Mr. Dorfschneider," Mama said.

He was carrying in a tray of pies, but he set them right down. "You think so?"

"For dinner last night, ve had some."

"Oh yeah?"

"Yes."

"I learned that from a great baker," he said in a soft voice. "My father." And then he was off on a long description of the way his father worked: of the way he never stinted on the number of eggs he dropped into the batter; the careful way he would examine apples when *his* suppliers showed up, picking samples out of the bushel baskets and cutting into them to make sure they met his standards of crispness and flavor.

After he was gone, Mama turned to me, and, pleased with herself or at least with the idea that she was teaching me about life, she said in Yiddish, "See? Every man has his good side."

"What do you mean?"

"Well, didn't you listen? He's full of respect for his papa."

I had been only half listening, and, influenced by my brothers, with the feeling that he sounded pompous and stupid, but I saw that to Mama this was an important change, somehow connected to the way we should feel about *our* papa. "He makes a good pie, too," I said.

She looked at me as if to say I hadn't gone quite far enough, but it would have to do. "I don't sell those Milton pies at all," she said.

The girls wanted to have the first meeting of the Jewish Girls Club at my house, which was both surprising and gratifying. "Okay, great," I said.

Part of the time we would discuss bylaws, but then we thought the appropriate thing was to have an activity. I knew exactly what we should do. By now the papers were so full of news about the war that even I was interested. Hadn't we had a special assembly on how evil the Germans were? Mr. Dunleavy, our principal, called them Huns and told us how they had cut off children's hands for stealing and chained their own soldiers to machine guns so they couldn't retreat.

It made us shudder to think about it. We could understand why, when people heard you had a German-sounding name, they looked at you with disgust.

"My Dad says this is the first time it's good to tell people you're a Jew," Sophie had said one day.

"Why?"

"When you got a name like Weingarten?"

"Or Klein," Toby had said. "Believe me, you don't want them thinking you're a Hun."

I had suddenly realized that Fried sounded German, also. Well, what better way to convince people we Jews were as American as they come than by knitting socks for the American soldiers going across the Atlantic to fight? Aunt Esther rolled her eyes when I told her. She wasn't as patriotic as she should have been. But the girls loved the idea.

They came over on Sunday. "This is great!" Toby

said as I distributed yarn and four sets of knitting needles and showed them how to get started.

We sat in the back, outside, concentrating as we did the first few rows, then able to talk as our fingers moved the needles automatically.

"What are the hunkies?" Blanche asked. "Are they Huns?"

"Hungarian," I said.

"No, I think they're Czechs. Papa says they're Czechs," Toby said.

"Well, my Papa said Hungarian."

There was a moment when nobody spoke. It seemed rude to argue with a dead man—as I had known when I brought it up.

"How's the store going?" Toby asked. Her father had a shoe store in downtown Harrisburg.

"Slow, but Uncle Izzie says don't worry, it's supposed to be slow."

"In the beginning, yeah."

"Dad says you have a good location. The last one in here, he didn't work out because he was a drunk."

"Do they let you help?" Blanche asked.

"Sometimes. I know how to work the register."

"Papa don't let me use our register," Toby said.

"Well, I don't use it much. Aunt Esther's there. And the boys."

"Oh, yeah. Heshie. He's cute," Sophie said.

I was amazed. I had started to look at boys, but I would never admit it to anyone. "You think so?"

Sophie took a final stitch, finishing off a row with a flourish, the way her mother finished a piece on their player piano. "Of course. Why else would we come to your house?"

Was that true? Or was this the kind of teasing that some kids thought passed for friendship? But she was smiling. I decided to take it as a joke.

Afterward, as I saw them out the door and came back in through the store, exhilarated by the success of the meeting, I thought I should tell Heshie. But when I saw him in the kitchen, sitting, chin in his fist, bent over his algebra homework, I changed my mind. Wouldn't he think it was silly of them—and sillier of me to mention it?

He looked up. "Meeting over?"

"Yeah."

"Go well?"

"Yeah. Very."

"What'd you talk about?"

"Nothing. Nothing special."

Eight

May turned into June. We were doing better. Each day during the fourth week we took in more than $22 and one day we hit $27, a record. But after the last day of the month, we all sat around as Joe and Jack did some figuring. We could tell it was bad. Neither one of them was smiling. "That's not enough," Jack said.

The problem was that suppliers had given us everything—every can of soup, every piece of candy, every pie, every egg, every cornflake—on credit. After we subtracted for rent and electricity and food for ourselves we hadn't sold enough to pay them back. Yet there were some things, like milk, that we had to keep on ordering.

"So far they haven't complained."

"They complain. They complain to Izzie."

Nobody argued with Mama. She had already made clear her reluctance to depend on him.

We were sitting in what had become our usual places after dinner: Rose and Gert on the floor in the living room, playing, Mama and the boys around the table, drinking tea in glasses, making plans, and I listening quietly on the couch.

"It's the best we've done," Heshie said.

"But it's not forty," Joe said.

"Jeez, Yussel. Forty. Even Izzie said we couldn't do that right away."

"It could take months," Heshie said.

"But we don't have months," Mama said.

Joe turned to Mama. "You mean if we're not averaging forty dollars by the end of the month, you want to close?"

"I don't know what I want," she said, sounding so depressed that even though Joe clearly wanted to continue, he let it drop. He watched her sip her tea in silence. "You know, in this country, most people, they drink tea from a cup," he said. He sounded angry.

Mama rose and walked to the cupboard over the sink, where we had a few china cups brought back by Papa from one of his peddling trips into the country. Taking one, she banged it down in front of Joe so hard that I thought it would crack. "Here. Try a cup."

Of course, not selling enough meant we had to pay our suppliers less. If nobody buys soup, you don't have to order more soup. But the next afternoon, Mama went to the bank and took twenty dollars from the savings we had sworn we wouldn't touch.

Each day after school, Harry and I went out with his fliers. GREAT DISCOUNTS!!! he had printed across the top. How could we cut our prices all the time? I asked him. He gave me a wink. Joe had set prices a little higher than normal, he said. So the discount just brought them back to what they should be. I told him he had a great future in business and hoped he would go into it the very day he got out of jail.

Thursday of the fifth week, I came home from school to find Mama sitting by the cash register, deep in conversation with a short, fat man with black hair pulled from the side of his head all the way across his bald top. He was our vegetable supplier, Mr. Throckmorton.

He looked disturbed when he saw me. He looked at Mama, raising his eyebrows and shoulders and gesturing toward me with his chin. I knew what that meant. She shook her head.

"Wehell, hello, little girl," he said to me, reaching out to stroke my head. To Mama he said, "You have a wonderful family, Miz Fried," and left.

The screen door squeaked shut behind him. We could hear the fading sound of his boots on the steps, then the grinding sound of his truck's motor.

"What did he want?"

Mama looked for a second as if she weren't going to tell me. Then she shrugged. "He's mad at Izzie for making him give us credit. He wants to be sure we pay him back the first of the month."

"Oh."

I knew she wasn't telling me the whole truth, and that made me angry. If she wasn't going to treat me as if I were old enough to hear bad news, why care? I went back into the house, where Heshie was counting out fliers. Aunt Esther was sitting on the floor with Rose and Gert, showing them a card game. I put away my things and returned to the store in case I could do something useful while I waited for Heshie. Mama was still sitting behind the register. Her cheeks were wet.

"What's wrong?"

She wiped her cheek with the side of her broad thumb. "I was thinking of Papa," she said in Yiddish, and I realized it was the first time I had thought about him in a while. Had I forgotten him already? So she wouldn't upset me, Mama jumped up, picked up a rag, and began dusting the glass countertops, her back to me.

Maybe this was what happened when people died. It affected you for a few weeks, and then you went back to doing your homework and folding laundry and trying to keep a store open. But I was upset. "Do you miss Papa?" I asked Heshie as we went out with our fliers.

"Oh yeah."

"What do you miss?"

"If he was around, he'd really know how to get this store moving."

"Oh."

He must have realized that wasn't the right answer. "I *miss* him. He was great," he said.

Saying what he thought he should say. In a way that made me feel better. If Heshie wasn't feeling bad, maybe I wasn't so terrible. And now I thought of another question. Why had Mama picked that moment to cry about Papa? It had seemed to me that she would be crying over the mean thing Throckmorton had said. Or was it that she missed Papa because at a time like this she wished he were around to *deal* with Throckmorton?

We crossed another street. We were getting farther away from our neighborhood now. It was about four-thirty. The streets were full of Hungarian women and kids, but there were no men around.

"All the hunkies work in the mill?" I asked.

"I guess they do." He didn't sound too sure. "Must be hard work."

"Ever see the muscles on those men? They're strong."

"Papa was pretty strong."

"Not like them," I said.

It was true. Papa was strong, but the hunky men

were a head taller than he was. "What do they do at the mill?"

"Oh, make steel," Heshie said. "Just . . . I don't know, exactly."

We walked on. I felt as if we were in a foreign country, walking past families whose men weren't peddlers or storekeepers or bookbinders.

Then, as we passed along the edge of the black section, I saw Roxanne, sitting on the wooden stoop of a house across the street. At first I pretended not to see her. But that didn't seem nice. I waved. She waved back.

I knew we should keep on walking. The problem was, I had waved too early. Now there was nothing to do but walk while the space between us narrowed, and continue to look at each other.

"There's somebody from my class," I said to Heshie. Without waiting for him I stepped into the street, lifting my feet high over the wagon-wheel ruts and the little pools of water trapped in them, then crossed over to say hello.

"Hi, Bertha. What you doing?" Roxanne said.

"Giving these out. It's about the store."

Behind her the door creaked open. A coffee-colored woman who looked about Jack's age came out onto the porch. "Who you talking to, Roxanne?"

"This girl in my class," she said. "And her brother."

The woman looked down at me. "You cute," she said. "Hi." She went back inside.

"That your sister?" I asked.

"My mama," Roxanne said.

"She looks young."

"She twenty-five."

"Where are your brothers?"

"They around," she said. "So you giving people these papers? Let me see."

80

I gave her one and watched her read down the page. "Nice." She handed it back. "You just giving it—" she waved across the street toward Hunkytown—"out there?"

We had been, of course. I hesitated. I could see Heshie behind her, nodding his head frantically.

But wouldn't telling her that hurt her feelings? Why *not* go into her neighborhood? It wasn't any farther away than streets we had been on twice in the last two days.

"No, we're doing these streets."

"You going in my neighborhood?"

"I guess? Aren't we, Heshie?"

He hesitated just the barest fraction of a second. "Sure," he said.

Roxanne jumped to her feet. "Well, hey," she said, "let me go with you."

It was the first time we had walked there. These people were poor! None of the houses were painted. There was a little patch of grass in front of each one, but the grass was brown or yellow, and there were no sidewalks; the grass ran down into the street. There were more people sitting on the porches than in Hunkytown. Most of them were kids, but there were mothers, too, some of them nursing babies, and there were more men. The men were standing on the corners, playing a game I had seen the older kids play in fields near our house, the one where you throw a knife into a square drawn on the mud. Some sat in front of the houses on packing boxes, with a bigger crate between them for a table, playing cards.

Roxanne walked between us. She seemed to know everybody. "Hi," she would call up to one of the porches. "These my friends, they got a store over on Third Street. Here's something about it." And either she would take a flier from Heshie or me and hand it over, or else Heshie would take it up onto the porch himself, stepping over the gaps where a step used to be, over a step so splintered it looked as if it would crack apart if you set foot on it.

Most of the grown-ups looked puzzled when we came up, but they were all friendly to Roxanne. They would study the flier carefully, the way grown-ups do when they want to show kids they're not humoring them. "That's not too far," they would say. Or: "Well, good luck." Or: "Well, thank you. That's good."

Heshie wasn't too happy, but he didn't say anything. He just wasn't talking at all. After about an hour, when our pack of fliers was getting small, he said to me: "Birdie, we gotta get home."

I was tempted to ask why. But it was late. "I guess we do," I said. We did one more street, and then we were out again by Roxanne's house.

"Well, see you in school," I said to her.

"Yeah. Guess so."

We turned to go. Then I turned back. "And, Roxanne. Thanks."

"We went to Niggertown!" Heshie said as we came bursting through the door past Aunt Esther, who was minding the store, and into the kitchen, where everybody had gathered before dinner.

"*Sha*," Mama said. "Never use that word. I mean that."

"Okay. But we did."

Pot roast was bubbling on the stove. The air was warm with the smells of carrots, potatoes, and meat.

Everybody crowded around. "What was it like?" Rose asked.

"Poor," Heshie said. He hadn't wanted to do those

streets, but now that we had, he couldn't wait to impress everybody with it.

"Did you go into the houses?"

"No. People were on the porches," I said.

"Vas safe?" Mama asked. She asked Heshie, not me.

"Course. Boy, are they poor."

"Some people say don't even serve them, Mama," Joe said.

"Dat is silly. Ve serve anybody has money."

"We have to," Jack said. The boys laughed.

When we all sat down to eat, the talk turned gloomy, though. We were doing better than that awful first week. Today it looked as if we would be over twenty-five dollars for the fifth day in a row. But by now even Rose knew that wasn't enough. "Yussel, is that near forty?"

"Not very, kiddo," he said.

"I can't figure out what else to do," Joe said. Before we had come back from New York, the uncles up there had all clapped him on the shoulder and told him he was the man of the house. It had made him very serious, and he wasn't smiling now. "We can't cut prices any more. We're lower than anybody. We can't raise prices. People around here are too poor."

"Vell dere's vun ting I do," Mama said.

"What's that?"

"Today, tree vimmin ask me for credit. I told them yes."

"You did?"

"I did. Birdie, look, I get vun of your notebooks. I keep a record."

"Ma, you *know* what Izzie said."

"Dese people been in here before. I trust dem."

"Did you tell them when to pay?"

83

"Last Friday in June," she said.

"How many families?" Jack asked.

"Tree."

"Well, if you're sure."

"I'm sure."

"It won't change things," said Joe. "Three families. Even ten families."

"It change for dem," Mama said.

"We went to a lot of houses today. Maybe we'll do better tomorrow," I said. I was changing the subject because I didn't like hearing them disagree.

"It won't happen tomorrow," Joe said. "Friday. People don't like to shop on Friday. Fridays we never do well."

"We don't do nothin'," Jack said.

"Why *is* that?" I asked.

"I don't know," Joe said. "We just don't."

Then the conversation became even gloomier. "Tell Heshie about Uncle Max," Joe said.

Everybody was silent. Mama sat for a few moments, seeming sorry Joe had brought up the matter. Esther, sitting next to her, got up, went over to the window above the sink where we put important papers, and brought back a postcard. She turned it over and passed it to Heshie. I could see the back, covered with Uncle Max's jagged handwriting. He had written in pencil, and it was smudged with erasures.

Heshie read it over.

"Can I see?"

He passed it to me with a look that said I was just a kid, but how could it hurt?

The news should have been welcome. Uncle Max and another brother had decided to enlarge their mill. That meant Mama could go up right away to work there if she wanted—and so could the boys. It was a solid offer of work. But I read it with a terrible, sinking feeling.

Of course she would take it! Uncle Max would be urging her to do it, and all her sisters, even Aunt Esther, would say it was the realistic thing to do. After all, she had tried the store and it wasn't working. Wouldn't she just smile and nod as they painted her a picture of life in New York, with a paycheck coming in and no suppliers to argue with? Of course she would!

I handed the postcard back to Heshie. The boys looked unhappy, too. At least I wasn't alone.

"Is the money good?" I asked.

"No. But is money."

"She won't go to jail," Jack said.

"Don't take the job, Mama. Please."

"I know how you feel," she said. "Vat choice do I have?"

"You have a choice. Uncle Izzie said he'll lend us money."

"But Max says—"

"Max says, Max says. Who cares what smelly old Max says. *We want to live here!*"

The silence after I was finished told me that even the boys thought I was wrong. I looked around. They were all staring at me: Jack with both hands on the table, as if he were on the verge of pushing himself away; Heshie while he curled and uncurled the postcard in his palm; Joe with his cup of tea halfway to his lips; Aunt Esther with her arms folded atop her massive chest. Everybody seemed frozen in attitudes of disapproval.

Only Mama didn't seem angry. "Uncle Max was always nice to you, Birdie. Remember all dose cones? You play with dose cones for hours and hours."

"There was nothing else to do," I said.

85

"Oh, yes dere vas."

"Come on, Birdie. Mama doesn't want to go up there any more than you do. We're all trying," Joe said.

"Not very hard," I said.

How could I have said all those things? On the other hand, what did I say that wasn't true? Why wasn't she willing to take Uncle Izzie up on his offer? All my old doubts about her were true, and that made me unwilling to do anything but glare at everybody, then get up and stomp out of the room.

I walked into the store, flicking on the overhead light, and pulled out my reader.

After a few minutes Aunt Esther came in and pulled up a stool beside me. I pretended to concentrate.

"Uncle Max isn't so smelly," she said.

"Yes, he is."

"Okay, a little smelly."

"He smells all the time."

"Okay, all the time, but not badly."

I looked up. "I see you're trying to make me feel better. Thank you very much, Aunt Esther, but it won't work."

"Why not?"

"Because I don't want to move back to New York. And Joe doesn't. And Jack doesn't. And Heshie doesn't. And—"

"And your Mama doesn't."

"How do you know?"

"Because we talk about it. I think that's all we talk about."

"She wants to move back."

"How do you know?" It was Aunt Esther's turn.

"She'd be close to all the sisters. Look, she doesn't care about roaches. She doesn't care about being near a river."

"No, she doesn't. But she cares because you care."

My anger was dying down. I was beginning to sound unreasonable, even to myself. "What do you think we should do?"

"Me? What does that matter?"

"You're part of the family."

She got up and put her arm around me, crushing me against her side. "I hope you believe that."

"We do. We all of us do."

"That's good for me to hear," she said.

We were standing by the cash register. Looking down I saw beside it a notebook I had bought last year, then never used. There was a pencil stuck in the pages.

"This is what Mama was talking about? The notebook?"

"Ya," Esther said.

"You can put a lot of names in that book," I said. Then I let her lead me back into the kitchen, where everybody was pretending I had never said a word.

Nine

Well, maybe things would get better. Maybe they would be wrong about Friday; maybe tomorrow all the mothers we had given our flier to would come pouring through the door.

On Friday, when I came home, there were some black women in the store. Some were alone. Some were with kids. They looked nervous, as if they expected to get kicked out. They would walk up and down the aisles slowly, looking at prices. Then they would come to the cash register with something small, usually under fifty cents.

I took my place behind the counter with Aunt Esther, pretending to do my homework. But I would look up every time somebody new came in, watching them until they were out of sight behind a counter.

Three times in a row, after paying, a woman started to leave, then turned back and asked, did we offer credit?

Each time Mama shook her head sadly. "No," she said.

"Okay. Thank you."

I could tell she was bothered. After the third time, she picked up the credit book with its few entries—less than a page. Attached to the book with a little piece of white string was a pencil. She wrapped the string around the book and put it under the counter. She didn't want the black people to see we were giving credit to white families.

"Why don't you give them the credit, too?" I asked at one point when the store had emptied out.

"I don't know," she said. "Everybody, dey say I shouldn't do."

That night, after dinner and shul, the mood was pretty cheerful. We couldn't touch money on the Sabbath, but we could talk about it. We'd done well for a Friday. Even without credit, the "coloreds" had added about five dollars to the day's receipts, and the boys were all full of compliments to me for having the idea to leaflet them.

Mama listened to them. Then she said, "I vant to know. Vy nobody give de colored credit?"

Jack said: "Just nobody does it."

"Most of the suppliers say we shouldn't even let them in the store," Joe said.

Mama threw her hands up in the air. "That's silly," she said, switching to Yiddish. "I know what that means. That's how they treated us in Russia. When I was a girl you couldn't go into stores even if you had a kopek or two. They wouldn't let us start a business. And they had all the same things to say about us. 'The Jews steal money.' 'You can't trust the Jews.' I don't have to listen to that. And I won't."

"I don't say I agree with it, Mama. I'm just telling you what people say," Joe said.

"We could do a new flier," Heshie said.

"What it would say?"

"That we'll give credit. We'll go back to Nig—to the colored houses and give them out. We can give them credit. I don't care."

"I don't know about that," Mama said. "Maybe I'll talk first with Izzie."

She soon got her chance. Sunday night, Izzie came over on one of the checkup visits that had become his habit. We were all sitting around the kitchen table, listening to him give us tips. He pointed to the table as if it were the one in his store. "Also very important," he said. "A table. In my store you see a table in front. Why this table?"

I could see everyone struggling to find an answer. "We don't know," Jack said.

"You see how is everything reduced? Bread, a day old, five cents. Pies, ten cents. Hats, some cockamamie salesman talked me into taking hats, twenty-five cents. Pipple see a bargain, dey buy, and I move de merchandise. You know who tought dat up? Mr. Voolvort."

After a second, I realized he meant Woolworth. "He a Jewish man, Volvort?" asked Mama.

"No. And a ganef," Izzie said. A thief. "But a smott ganef."

Uncle Izzie was in a good mood. But when Mama asked him her question, he began shaking his head even before she got all the words out of her mouth. *Credit to the colored?* It was bad enough she was doing it at all. If the suppliers heard about it they would be angry. And there was another thing. The mills wouldn't like it.

Of all the workers, he said, the colored were the heaviest users of the company stores. To start luring them away would deprive the mills of a lot of money. And they

90

would get angry not just at our store but at everybody, he said. Although they probably wouldn't do anything about it. After all, this was America.

I understood what Uncle Izzie was saying. We had grown up on stories about Russia, where Jews were usually allowed to open only the kinds of businesses the Russians didn't want. In contrast to our neighborhood in Brooklyn, where half the store signs were in Hebrew, this town had just a few Jews—that was particularly clear at Christmastime, when most people had trees in their living rooms. It was easy to imagine that our grocery store could be taken away from us on a moment's notice. Although America *was* wonderful, we couldn't be sure it was safe.

"I see," Mama said. During the rest of the dinner, she hardly said a word.

The next afternoon, I came home from school and went into the store. Mama was behind the cash register. I took my usual place on a high-backed stool, took out my arithmetic book, and began doing long division. Heshie was behind the counter, grinding coffee and tying the bags with little pieces of twine.

There were two or three women in the store, walking up and down with wicker baskets on their arms. Two were white. One was a black woman I recognized from when Heshie and I had delivered leaflets.

A truck pulled up in front with a squeal of brakes and a horrific grinding of gears that we all recognized. Dorfschneider. In he came, making his afternoon delivery. He put down a box containing loaves of bread, then went back outside and came in with another box. I looked back at my book.

"Hey! What's this?"

I looked up. Dorfschneider had grabbed the black woman's wrist. She was holding a loaf of bread. "What do you think you're doing?"

"I'm seeing if it fresh," she said. She looked frightened.

"You got some nerve. Put that down."

She dropped the bread.

"Now get out of here."

She started to walk toward the door, looking scared.

But as she walked down the aisle, Mama moved out from behind the counter to block her way. "Vait," she said, looking past the woman at Dorfschneider. "Vy you do dat?"

He looked at Mama as if amazed that she would ask. "You can't let them handle the merchandise."

"Everybody does."

"White people. Christian people." Then, remembering, "And Hebrew."

Dorfschneider was an important supplier, and we owed him money. Besides, since the day Mama had complimented his pies, he had seemed to soften toward us. Mama's lips were compressed. I could see she was mad. But she hesitated. "Oh," she said. She turned to the woman. "Vas fresh?"

"Yes."

"Tek it home. No charge," she said.

I'll never forget the look on Dorfschneider's face. He looked hurt, as if Mama had rejected a favor. But then he snorted. He turned and clumped out of the store. We listened to the truck start up, grind into gear, and pull off.

Mama turned to Heshie. He was standing with a bag of coffee in his hand. "Heshie," Mama said.

"Yes, Mama."

"I have for you a job. I vant a new—vat you call it?"

"Flier?"

"Flier. Dat's it."

Up and down the streets we went with the new flier, which looked much like the old one except for one sentence, circled in thick red pencil. It had been worked out by Heshie, Jack, and Joe after endless debate and revision around the dining room table: CREDIT GIVEN TO RESPONSIBLE CUSTOMERS!!!

We didn't see Roxanne outside her house. I can't say we felt comfortable heading down the streets where the black families lived, just the two of us. But we could do it. For an hour we went up and down, splitting up the sides of the streets.

"Tell people about the credit. Point it out," Heshie told me.

"Even with that red pencil?"

"Not everybody can read," he said.

I was sure this wasn't true, but didn't want to make him feel ignorant. If there was an adult on the porch or in the street, I pointed to the line, saying, "And we're giving credit to responsible customers," hoping they wouldn't ask me questions about it.

Nobody did. The men seemed to stop listening as soon as I started. But the women would nod, then take the fliers, fold them up carefully, and put them in their dress pockets.

And the next day they began coming in. There weren't many—maybe four or five women walked up the steps and through the screen door, holding the flier, pointing to the words and asking, "You giving credit?" As if they thought we'd changed our minds.

"Ve give," Mama would say.

"How long?"

"End of the month."

"How much credit you giving?"

"Five dollars," Mama would say firmly, to show there was no bargaining.

They might nod a few times, thinking it over. Then they'd pick up one of the wicker baskets and set off down the aisle.

Usually they bought a dollar, or two dollars' worth at a time. They bought flour and eggs, milk, coffee, sugar. They didn't buy many of the canned goods. But they bought a lot of milk. They would come carrying battered aluminum pitchers or wooden buckets. Mama or Aunt Esther would stick the ladle down into the barrel, swirl it around, then ladle the milk into the pitchers or buckets until they were full.

Undoubtedly there were families too afraid of the mill-owners to use us. In fact, sometimes people would make nervous little jokes about it as they waited at the counter. But by the third day, twenty families had crossed over into our neighborhood to buy at the store. By the end of that week, the sixth since we opened, it was forty, and they were coming back. Each time they bought, one of us would get out the credit book, find their name, and mark down the items, as well as the total cost.

By the end of the week, Jack and Joe were worried. "You know how much we've sold on credit?" Jack asked.

"How much."

"A hundred twenty dollars. That's thirty a day."

"And it's getting bigger every day," Joe said.

"Is vundaful," Mama said.

"Only if we get paid back," Jack said.

"Are ve getting new families?"

"Some."

"I see people coming back," I said.

Nobody paid attention to me. "People are coming back," Heshie said as if I hadn't said a word.

"I hope they keep comink," Mama said.

"Ma, this is serious. It means we've got to order a lot more for next week. It means Dorfschneider will be carrying us. We'll be in the hole hundreds of dollars."

"I know. I know, Yussel. I vorry about it, too."

The days were warm now. The leaves were out on the trees. In the morning, the fields were dry when we walked to school and we didn't even bring sweaters. At night it was no longer dark after dinner. We had time to clear the dishes, do our homework, then go outside to watch the sparks and flame spewing from the mill stacks as the sun, sinking below the houses to the west, turned the sky orange and purple.

For Joe and Jack there were finals, but for the rest of us school was winding down. Miss Cleary had trouble getting us to concentrate during afternoon classes—especially the boys. There were times when even I found myself staring out the big windows at the blue sky, thinking about the last day, when teachers would collect the books and we could walk out of the building knowing we didn't have to wake up early or think about long division until fall.

On Monday in school, Roxanne came up to me before class.

"How your store goin'?"

"Good."

"My mama say she like it."

"I saw her in there."

"Yeah. It much better than the mill store."

"Oh. Your Dad works at the mill?"

"Yeah."

I knew that it must have made Roxanne nervous to go up and talk to a white girl—even a Jewish girl—without being spoken to first. And to say something nice about the store! At the end of recess, I was talking to Sophie. But when we lined up to go inside, I lined up with Roxanne. We went in together.

Uncle Izzie sounded completely exasperated. *"Mit zeine meshugassen veht ehr zich bagroben,"* he said, sitting on a milk box in the kitchen Monday night—with your craziness, you'll dig your own grave.

We were finished with dinner. Joe and Heshie were already doing homework. Jack and Esther were in the store. I was playing with Gert and Rose by the stove.

Mama pulled a chair over to him and sat down on it. She said something to him, almost in a whisper.

He shook his head again. "I cover for you avile," he said. Clearly, he didn't care if we heard. "But credit to the coloreds? Vat if Dorfschneider, who you can see he's a meshuggener, vat if *he* don't like it?"

"*Nu*. Who says they have to know?"

He laughed. "Rivka, you are— You got noive. You got a good heart. But also you need a good head." There was no anger in his voice, though.

Ten

There was a big lot about two blocks away from the store. It was near the school, on a street that contained only one house. A sign attached to two posts driven into the grass read CONSTRUCTION PLANNED: MCLENEHAN AND LUCAS CONST. CO.

The sign had been there as long as we'd been in the neighborhood. On this day, though, a bright, sunny Tuesday, I walked by to see the lot swarming with dark-skinned men, hunkies or Italians (we had no nickname for the Italians). A bulldozer was grinding its way along the road, and men on two big steam shovels were excavating and loading dirt into two big trucks and a horse-drawn cart.

When I came into the store, filled with importance and anxious to tell everyone about it, it turned out everybody knew.

"They were all in here at lunchtime," Esther said. "They wanted sandwiches."

Did we sell sandwiches? We hadn't planned on it, but why not? These men might be working there for six months. By the next morning, Aunt Esther had set up a wooden table, next to the cold-meat section, with mustard and waxed paper and piles of napkins. Presto. We were in the sandwich business. The only problem was that at lunchtime, when they trooped in again, most of them wanted ham.

"What did you do?" I asked that afternoon.

"I try to sell them roast beef."

"Did they buy it?"

"Some."

She shrugged as if to tell me she could live with it. But by the end of the week it had become a daily exercise in frustration. At noon the men would troop in, ordering sandwiches and soda. By now a lot of them knew. But somebody would always ask for ham and Swiss. Esther would explain that we didn't carry ham, being Jewish. They would laugh and order something else: roast beef or egg salad. But by Friday the number of men was clearly dropping off.

"Maybe they're bringing lunch from home," Heshie said that night.

"Or maybe goink someplace else."

"Where? There's nobody within a mile of here sells sandwiches."

Aunt Esther was sitting, her chair pushed away from the table so she could spread her fat legs, her skirt stretched between them like a flowered hammock. "I say sell the garbage," she said in Yiddish. "There's a big difference between eating it and selling it."

"Esther!" Mama said. "Louie would never have allowed such a thing."

"That's Louie. And who knows. Maybe he'd see the gentiles want it and change his mind."

"I couldn't."

"Frankly, I don't see any problem," I said loftily. "We're not eating it."

Mama looked at me as if I had lost my mind.

"Birdie," Heshie said.

I figured I had missed something and shut up.

But Thursday afternoon, as I sat in back of the register—this time drawing a map of Pennsylvania from memory and labeling the ten largest towns—one of the hunky women came in. She looked through the glass at the meats and said, "A nize ham? You got one?"

"Ve not sell ham," Esther said.

"Vy not? You no got five-pound ham, veddy nize?"

Mama shook her head sorrowfully. "You vant, maybe, roast bif? Five pounds? Veddy gut?"

"Vat?"

"Roast bif."

I held my breath. Five pounds was a big sale. The woman shook her head. "No, no. I vant a ham."

She left. For a while we were all silent. Aunt Esther looked at Mama, waiting for her to say something. She didn't. Finally Esther said, "Look, darling. Izzie sells ham."

"He's not religious."

"He's religious. He belongs to a temple. Look, you order it, I handle it. The whole thing."

"This you're willing to do?"

"I handle garbage every day," Esther said, looking like she wanted to spit. "If they want to eat garbage, I can slice it for them."

And so the next day, after one phone call to Franklin, the meat man, we had ham. Sliced ham. Cooked ham. Smoked ham. Tins of Virginia ham on the shelves. It was a hit, Mama told us when we came in from school. A few minutes later, we all looked on with some amazement when a customer came in, ordering two pounds of the stuff, sliced. Esther went to the meat cabinet, picked up the greasy, square hunk of pig, and sliced off two pounds, letting it fall onto a sheet of white butcher paper as calmly as if it were a hunk of cheddar cheese.

"I still don't see how you can do that," Mama murmured in Yiddish after the customer left—there were still some people in the store.

Esther smiled. It was as if she had been complimented for being tough. She wiped her hands on a paper towel and dropped it into the trash. Then she went over to the sink and washed, just the way she would have if she had been handling garbage. "They have the ham. We have eighty cents," she said.

It was the eighth week we were open and the last week of the month—the week all the credit accounts came due. On Monday and Tuesday I came home from school to find the store filled with customers. I don't mean that there were lines at the cash register. Nothing like that. But in every aisle there were one or two women, wicker baskets over their arms, picking things off the shelves. About half of them were white, the other black. Business was so steady we didn't dare let the store go unattended, not even during dinner. Only around nine, when Gert and Rose were asleep and I was getting ready for bed, would we all gather around the table, watching Joe count up the day's receipts.

"Forty-two dollars, fifty-two cents," Joe said one night.

"Vundaful," Mama said.

"Yay," I said.

"What about without what's in the credit book?" Jack said.

Joe looked down for a second. "Thirty-one something."

100

"That's not so good."

"Is good," Mama said. "Dese is nice people."

"Maybe they're nice, maybe they're not. Even nice people don't pay their bills."

"What do we do if they don't?" Heshie asked.

I felt as if he had attacked my friends. "We'll go to the houses and ask them for it," I said.

The boys all hooted. "You and who else?" But there was no ridicule in it. Since I had had the idea to go into Roxanne's neighborhood they had treated me almost like one of them.

"I'll go myself. With Roxanne," I said, giving them another reminder.

"Ve can do zat?" Mama asked, turning to Heshie.

He shrugged. "Who knows."

The next morning I walked through the black iron gates of the school just as everyone was lining up. Sophie and Toby were already ahead of me. I wound up standing next to Roxanne.

"I'm scared," she said.

"Why?"

"I done lost my stockings."

I looked down. Sure enough, her brown legs were bare right down until they disappeared into her worn, scuffed shoes.

"How could you lose your stockings?"

She looked ashamed. "Well, actually, I didn't lose them. I ripped them on a nail. It looked so awful, I just pulled them off and put them in my book bag."

"Maybe you should've left them on."

"Either way, she goin' to yell at me."

"She won't be so bad," I said.

"Oh, yes, she will. She don't like me when I got *new* stockings."

"No. It happened to Blanche once. She won't do anything."

"Sh," said one of the girls in front.

Miss Cleary was circling us in her usual way, pausing as she came along the line to tell Philip Djilas, a boy best known for drawing pictures of naked girls in chalk on the sidewalk, that he had missed a loop with his belt. He unbuckled it, stripped it off, and began slipping it through the holes.

She came abreast of us and went by. Then she stopped. She backed up a pace. "Oh, Roxanne," she said, "your legs are bare."

Looking at Miss Cleary, I expected to hear Roxanne offer her excuse. But she was silent. I glanced at her. Her head was down. She was looking at the ground, studying her shoes as if looking for some solution in the yellow, scuffed leather of her shoe tops.

"Don't you know you must come to school neatly attired?"

"Yes'm."

"Do you perhaps think because school is ending I'll be lax about the rules?"

"No, ma'am."

"Do you have stockings?"

"Miz Cleary, they got ripped."

"Got ripped. By magic?"

"No'm."

"Well, what should I do? What should *you* do about this?"

Silence.

"Well, I think we should send you home for the day. Or until you come back correctly attired."

"That's mean," I said.

I could see Toby's head whip around.

Miss Cleary turned to me. "Do you want me to send you home as well, Bertha?"

"No, Miss Cleary."

"Then keep your thoughts to yourself. Go on, Roxanne. You go home now."

I could see tears rolling down Roxanne's face, but nobody else could. After a moment she began to move off. I could see kids in the other lines looking around curiously. I sneaked a last look at Roxanne walking out through the gate, then turned my eyes front as we marched through the big wooden doors and into the hallway of the school.

What a stupid thing to do, especially in front of Toby and Sophie and Blanche! I braced myself as they converged on me during recess.

If I had any hope that I had misjudged them, it vanished as soon as I saw Sophie, shaking her head, her eyebrows lifted and mouth tugged to one side. "God, how could you *do* it?" she said.

"Do what?"

"You know. Stick up for a—" She looked at Toby.

"A nigger," Toby said. She had no qualms about the word.

"Right, a nigger," Sophie said.

"Well, it was mean."

"Why? She broke a rule."

"She's not the only one."

"Oh, are you referring to me?" Blanche said. "Am I the one to whom you refer?"

"You know you are."

"That was totally different. Totally."

"How?"

"Birdie," Sophie said. "Come on. You're not going to continue to tell us you did the right thing, are you?"

"I don't believe it," Toby said. "Do you believe it?"

"No, I don't believe it," Sophie said. "Especially that you'd do this to your friends."

"Do *what* to my friends?"

"You know."

"I *don't* know."

"Now people see how rotten Jews are. They say, 'Oh, here is this kid makes friends with the worst sort of people.' It gives all of us a bad name."

"Right, right. Birdie, people don't say 'Oh, it was just Birdie.' They think it's all Jews."

I was stunned. Put that way, I really had done something wrong.

Well, so what! Wrong as it was, weak as I was, I couldn't help feeling that way about Roxanne. But I was on the verge of tears; suddenly I was afraid to say much more for fear that I would totally lose control, and I hated that thought so much I jumped to my feet. "Well, that's the biggest bunch of nonsense I ever heard and if you don't like it you can stuff it up your nose." And I walked off so quickly it was clear there was no use trailing after me.

To make matters worse, I had walked off without any sense of where I was going. I found myself heading for the brick wall where the boys were playing kick ball. I veered away, still walking fast, thinking I would go inside and sit in the bathroom, when I saw Heshie coming over.

"Hi."

"Hi."

"I heard you got into trouble."

"How'd you hear that?"

"Oh, one of the sixth graders came over and told me. 'Did you hear about your crazy sister?' That kind of thing."

"And you probably said, 'Yeah, she's crazy.' "

"Now, why would I say that?"

"You don't like Roxanne. You didn't even want to give her a flier."

"Well, I was wrong about that."

"You were?"

"Sure. I don't have nothing against the colored. I don't know why they live the way they do, but some of them seem fine. Roxanne seems fine. Only thing I was worried about was you getting into trouble with Cleary."

"What would she do?"

"Give you a B instead of an A. But don't worry. If that happens, I'll explain it to Mama."

And then, right in the middle of the playground, with kids walking back and forth, and his own friends standing in little knots by the wall of the school, Heshie put his arm around me, his little sister, bent down, and gave me a kiss.

What more could you ask of a brother? I watched him walk back to his friends. Then I walked off myself, not sure where to go, but content to be alone.

I could see Blanche and Toby and Sophie sitting by themselves by the fence, legs curled up under them, their dresses spread out, deep in conversation. Well, what if they wouldn't be my friends? What if they decided to continue the JGC without me? I would just find new friends—maybe hunkies. Maybe even Roxanne.

I sat down by myself, pretending great interest in a

squirrel scurrying below one of the oak trees outside the fence.

The bell rang. The ball games stopped and kids separated into their classes to begin lining up to go inside. I stood up, too.

As I did, I saw Roxanne come through the school gate. She was wearing her stockings, a big rip in one of them sewn up with white thread. For a second I thought I should ignore her, and go do what I usually did, line up with Blanche and Toby or Sophie. But how could I possibly do that after what they had said?

I walked up to Roxanne, who was standing alone at the end of the line. "I see you're correctly attired," I said.

"I guess."

We stood side by side while Miss Cleary came by. I wondered if she would object to the white thread. But maybe she had thought better of what she had done. She stopped during inspection and, in a soft voice, said, "Better, Roxanne."

Eleven

That night in the store, Heshie told Mama, as if it were something she ought to know. She listened to the story and said, "Don't get into trouble." She put her arms around me and hugged me to her chest. And then she went back to something important: wiping clean the glass windows of the candy and meat cases.

The next night, Thursday, was the night before credit payments were due, and everyone was nervous.

"We have $173 on the books," Joe said after the store closed. "If they pay us, great. If not, we're sunk."

One hundred seventy-three dollars! Mama's entire savings were less than ninety dollars. Sitting there and listening to the boys argue, I could see there was something to worry about. And to make matters worse, tomorrow would be *Shabbes*.

Joe asked, "Ma, can't we keep the store open late?"

No, she said. What difference would that make? We would do what we always did: Mama and Esther and I would clean the house. Mama would cook. We'd close at sundown, and have chicken and flanken as usual. We wouldn't handle money until Saturday night. If there were a few stragglers, they could wait.

Heshie got permission to stay home on Friday. He knew English better than Mama or Esther, and Mama wouldn't feel comfortable, anyway, trying to mark up the credit book while they handled a rush of customers, all speaking a funny English that she still found hard to understand.

So the next morning Rose and I set off to school by ourselves. It was the day when I finally understood kids who said they hated school. There was a round electric clock over the blackboard. Its big hand didn't move until the minute was up, when it would jerk forward with a click so loud that during tests it could make you jump. Each time it clicked I would look up, hoping I had missed a click, that more than a minute had passed. But it never had.

Oh, I wanted that day to be over! Wouldn't it be great to run inside the store and see the women lining up at the cash register with real cash money? Or to get the job of sitting with the credit book, finding each name as Mama called it off, putting my finger under the amount, reading it off, then writing *paid* and making a big circle around it with the stubby pencil we kept on the counter?

At recess, I brought my reader out with me. I saw Blanche and Toby and Sophie already out on the playground, playing jacks. I made myself look away. I picked out a spot as far from them as it was possible to get, and opened my book.

As I sat, trying to concentrate, a shadow fell on my book. I looked up. It was Sophie.

"Hi."

"Hi."

"Can I sit down?"

"Suit yourself."

She sat.

"Where are the others?"

"I don't know. Well, I do know. They didn't want to come over."

"Why not?"

"Because I wanted to say I was sorry for what I said yesterday."

Could anything be more exhilarating? "What was that?"

"You know. About Roxanne."

"Oh. You mean you don't think it was stupid?"

"No. Dangerous. Not stupid."

"What's so dangerous about it?"

"Cleary could kill you."

"She's not so tough," I said.

"Tough enough. Anyway, I decided it wasn't dumb. I think it was kind of nice of you."

"Well, thanks."

"So, can we still be friends?"

"What? Oh, sure."

"Good," she said.

I looked back down at my book. She sat for a minute, hoping I might say something. Finally, she stood up. "See ya," she said, moving away.

"Bye," I said, still looking at my book. I was sure the four of us would never be friends again.

After school I didn't hang around. I just went up to Rose, said, "Come on," and headed home as fast as she could walk. And it wasn't until we had turned the corner onto our street and started toward the store that I had any idea that something might be going wrong. The tip-off: Nobody was coming either in or out. Heshie was

109

sitting on the steps. He saw us and waved, kind of halfheartedly. Then he looked away in the other direction, as if he were expecting somebody.

I started running. "Wait for me," Rose called, but I was too eager. "How are we doing?" I asked Heshie.

"Terrible."

"People aren't paying up?"

"Maybe twenty dollars. Just a usual Friday."

"How come?"

"I don't know. Nobody can figure it out."

There was one customer in the store, a Hungarian woman with a gold front tooth, waiting while Mama sliced some roast beef and wrapped brown paper around it. I knew Mama wouldn't want me to say anything in front of the woman. "Hi," I said.

"Hi."

Rose came in, crying that I had left her behind.

Aunt Esther got up off the stool by the cash register. "Sh," she said to Rose. "Have some candy."

She did that only when she wanted to shut us up. The woman paid and left, letting the door slam behind her. "What's going on?" I asked.

"I don't know," Mama said in Yiddish. She looked as if she were going to cry.

Aunt Esther was just sitting on the high-backed stool, looking down into her smudged apron. "Nobody come," she said in English. "Maybe is all a trick." She pulled the credit book out from under the register and handed it to me. I looked down the page. Maybe five of the forty families had their names circled.

It *was* a trick! These people had taken advantage of us, immigrants, strangers to the town. They would run up big bills. Then they would just go someplace else. For all I knew, maybe they would even move to another town. When we came knocking on their doors, we'd just find some new family, who would tell us they didn't know a thing!

When I offered this possibility, the women barely answered. "Who knows," Mama said finally. She was trying to make me feel better.

"What do we do?"

She sat, thinking for a few seconds. Then she kind of pulled herself together. "We clean the kitchen and living room, as always. When we close we light the candles, as we always do. And Saturday night we sit and count up how much we owe and figure it out."

"But—"

"And cleaning, that means you. Get going."

"Do I have to?"

"Yes."

"I hate cleaning."

"So do I."

"But the boys—"

"Birdie!"

I stopped. I had never heard such a tone from her. "Yes?"

"Do it."

"Yes, Mama."

I walked sullenly through the store, put my books down, and picked up the broom.

My job was to sweep and mop the kitchen floor, wax the table, then sweep the rest of the house. For the next hour and a half I would spend ten minutes at a time working, then find some excuse for going back into the store to see if anything had changed.

Nothing had. Heshie was right. There was only the

usual light Friday afternoon crowd: a few hunky women with baskets going up and down the aisle, occasionally one of the black women coming in to make a small purchase—a loaf of bread, a pitcher of milk—and counting out the few nickels from a knitted change purse. I would walk in as if I had an errand, look around, then suddenly change direction as if I'd forgotten something, and walk back into the house.

Finally, when I had finished cleaning, I brought a book into the store and took my place behind the counter. After a while Joe and Jack drifted in. Joe wasn't working that day but there had been a meeting at the high school. Both of them took a look at the book, listened to Mama's description of the day, then picked out some chore to do, looking worried.

At one point, when the store was completely empty, I asked, "Mama, what do we do if nobody pays?" I felt like a sick person who asks the doctor if she's going to die.

Mama swiveled around to look at me. "We close up the store. Move back to New York. I go to work for Uncle Max."

"But why?"

"Because we owe so many people."

"But Izzie would help!"

"Izzie helped enough. It's time to pay him back."

"Couldn't you get a job here?"

"Where?"

I said the first thing that came into my mind. "Maybe working in the mill. Jack and Joe could do that."

"My boys don't work in a mill," she said coldly.

Well, wasn't that up to them? They didn't want to go back to New York, either! But I was too intimidated by her tone to say anything else. I just sat there, feeling chastised.

Once in a while a customer would come in. Mama would smile warmly and say something about what a nice day it was. Jack and Joe would get up and pretend to have some boxes to unpack, smiling at the customer and saying cheerful things to each other with the kind of warmth you'd reserve for a long-lost cousin.

I couldn't even pretend to be cheerful. I imagined how it would happen: the CLOSED sign strung over the door; people walking by, surprised there were no lights, peering in to see if there were signs of life. What would Mama do to pay off the suppliers? Or would we not pay them off, and leave with our suitcases for the train station in the middle of the night like thieves?

No, probably Izzie would help us a little more. But eventually we would pack up, and movers would come, and we would be on the train to New York again, sitting silently the way we had just six weeks before.

And now another thought struck me. Wasn't this all my fault? Sure it was! Whose idea had it been to go into Roxanne's neighborhood? Whose idea to talk to Roxanne? Whose idea to give out the fliers? And who had been so confident, and talked about going to people's doors to get them to pay back what they owed? I had been so conceited, thinking my idea had saved us! In fact, it was just the reverse.

"Birdie, go out and play," Mama said. She said it kindly, and I was immediately suspicious. Could she read my thoughts? Was she trying to convey by her tone that she wasn't angry for what I had done?

I couldn't stay there anymore. I walked outside to where Heshie was still sitting on the step.

"Well, back to New York," he said.

"It makes me so mad. Where's Roxanne's mom?"

"She might come."

"Yeah, her. But where's everybody else?"

"These are poor people," he said, and I knew he was echoing something he must have heard from Mama. "Maybe they don't have the money. Look, New York won't be so bad. You'll have Ruthie."

"Sure, and a bathroom full of cockroaches. They're *disgusting*."

He looked at me as if trying to decide whether he should argue. "You don't have to hang around here. Why don't you go over Sophie's? Maybe you'll feel better."

"No," I said slowly. "I can't go there anymore."

"Oh, yeah," he said. "I forgot."

Then, since neither of us knew what more to say, we fell silent. After a while Heshie stood, just to do something, and we went back inside to sit by the window. Nobody was talking. But we were all conscious of the clock on the back wall, silently moving. 6:10. 6:30. 7:00.

At twenty to eight, with the sun low in the horizon, Mama said, "Let's close up."

"Can't we stay open a little longer?" Heshie pleaded.

"It's *Shabbes*."

"But—"

"No buts. Ve close."

We all stood, Esther slowly lifting herself off the stool behind the meat counter, Heshie and me off the packing box by the front window. Mama pulled out the CLOSED sign from under the counter, passing it over to Heshie.

And so it was that Heshie, opening the door and peering out a little as he slipped the sign over the outside door handle, was the one who saw them. "Here's your friend," he said. "Here's Roxanne."

I jumped to my feet. Through the glass I saw Roxanne and her mother mounting the steps and pushing inside past Heshie, who stood politely to one side. "Hi, Miz Fried," said Roxanne. "We came to pay what we owe."

Mama made herself smile. She stood and got the credit book.

"You're about the only one," Heshie said.

Roxanne looked at him, blinking, as if it were taking awhile to grasp what he had said. "Well, they be comin' in," she said. She sounded a little insulted. Or maybe she was afraid we'd be angry. We were Jews but we were still white people. "Everybody waitin' till they get paid."

"What?" Heshie said, moving closer.

"Why, sure. The mill, they pay every Friday. Then you got to get that scrip changed. They coming."

Finally we understood why Fridays had always been such light days. It had just never occurred to us.

"You mean that's why nobody's been by?" Heshie asked.

"You ain't had *no*body by?"

"No."

"Well, I'll bet that's why."

And as if to make us believe it, the door opened. Another woman walked in, Mrs. Washington, who had the largest bill on the books.

"Miz Fried. Hello, boys."

Heshie ran to the door. "There's more coming down the street!" he said, his voice barely under control.

I ran to look. It wasn't a mob. It was one woman, then a couple more, and then, rounding the corner, a man still in work clothes. They began coming up the steps and into the store. Soon there were about ten people there, half of them black, half hunky, the groups not talking to each other, but not seeming to mind being in the store together, and all with a cheery greeting for us, and the store was packed.

"I told you," Roxanne said to Heshie over the din.

My heart was pounding. I didn't trust myself to speak. I smiled at her even though she wasn't looking at me. I wanted to make sure she thought we were a friendly family. I moved up next to Roxanne so people would remember this was partly my idea, then was ashamed at my greediness for taking credit. The boys were smiling, too, and hitting each other on the shoulder and looking out the windows to see how many people were coming. "There's more!" Heshie said, like a lookout in one of his William S. Hart movies.

Mama was busy ringing up payments at the register. Jack was handling the credit book. At one point he looked up and saw me standing with Roxanne. He smiled at me, then went back to writing. And things would have been perfect if I hadn't had the terrible impulse to look at the clock.

"Mama, it's after eight!" I said.

"Let's stay open!" Joe said.

Mama looked up at the clock. The noise in the store made her nervous. "No. We close," she said in Yiddish.

"And turn everybody away?"

For a few seconds she didn't answer. "Yes."

"What's wrong?" Roxanne's mother asked.

Jack explained that it was the Jewish Sabbath, that once the sun set we weren't allowed to handle money. I could tell he was gritting his teeth. Would everybody go away and come back? Was he going to have to wait until Sunday to see what would happen?

Roxanne's mom said, "Well, get one of us to do it."

116

"You mean take the money?" Jack asked. "You'd do that?"

"Why, sure. This store is good for us. Your prices are good. You give us credit. We never had a store do that before. And"—she looked around until her eyes found mine—"Miz Fried, you have a very nice daughter. A *fine* daughter. You a fine *family*."

The customers looked puzzled. The family was looking at me, beaming, even Jack and Joe.

"Teng you," Mama said.

"But do you know how we do this?" Jack said. "Looking up the names. Crossing everybody's name off the books." He held up the credit book, the pencil dangling by the white string.

"Well, I can't read," Mrs. Johnson said, seeming a little embarrassed. Jack's face fell. "But Roxanne here, she can."

In case she hadn't been following, Jack explained this to Mama in Yiddish. She looked at Mrs. Johnson for a few moments. Then she broke into a smile. "Teng you," she said. "Tengs very much."

Twelve

And that was what happened. For the next hour and a half, Mrs. Johnson stood behind the cash register, explaining to the customers that this was the Hebrew Sabbath. We didn't like being called Hebrews, but we didn't correct her. We just smiled at everybody. She would take the money. Roxanne would find the right name in the book. Sometimes she had a little trouble reading the writing, which after all was usually Mama's. Jack would look at Mama to check if it was all right, then point out the right name. He did it quickly, as if he were afraid Papa might see.

Did we think we had to do this? That if we didn't the families wouldn't come back? Probably not. But who could tell? Of course, to be truly observant we should have left the store, had our dinner, and gone to shul. But we couldn't. Not even Mama could. At one point she sent me back into the house to check the soup. The chicken was already falling apart. We were hungry. But we stayed in the store until every family had come, paid, and left. It was almost 9:30 before the store was empty and quiet again, empty that is, except for our family, Roxanne, and Roxanne's mom.

"Whoa. That was *busy*," Roxanne said. She sat down on the stool.

The rest of us stood around, nobody knowing what to say. For an hour all the shyness and the differences in our stations in life had been erased by the sheer busyness of collecting money. But now, in the quiet, the awkwardness came back.

We kept smiles on our faces, though. And then Mama said to Roxanne's mother: "This vas very nice ting you do. Tang you. You veddy nice pipples."

It took Mrs. Johnson a second to decipher what she had said. Then she smiled. "I glad we could do it."

"You vant maybe some chicken?"

"No, no, no. We be getting back."

Mama looked around. She knew there was something more she should say but she didn't know how to express it. Then she strode over to the candy jars. She stuck her hand in and pulled out a fist full of licorice sticks and dots and little chocolates wrapped in silver. She held these out to Roxanne. "For you," she said.

The minute Roxanne and her mother left, we practically danced our way through the flowered linoleum hallway leading to the kitchen.

"Two hundred six!" Jack said, reaching behind him to untie the soiled butcher's apron and flinging it onto one of the chairs."

"What's that? Two hundred six what?" I asked.

"That's how much we took in," Heshie said. "Right?"

"Right."

"Whoo!" Heshie said. "And, Birdie, you did this." He looked at me with a smile I had seen only once before, when he had kissed me on the playground. "It was the colored people did this." He reached out to put an arm around my neck.

What was the point of being a hero if you couldn't express disapproval of your older brothers—especially if you were right?

"You're not supposed to know it's two hundred six. It's *Shabbes*. You can't count the money on *Shabbes*," I said.

"I did it in my head," Jack said. "What's it say in the Bible about that?"

"I don't think Papa would like it," I said. We were all in the kitchen now. I looked at Mama so she could back me up.

"Like what?"

"Jack was keeping track of the money in his head," I said.

"And you think Papa wouldn't like that?"

"Well, would he?"

She smiled. "Maybe, maybe not," she said. "How much money?"

"Two hundred six," Heshie and Joe said, almost together.

She turned to them. "Two hundred six?" she said in Yiddish, to make sure.

"And twenty-two cents," Jack said.

"What's our average?" Heshie asked.

"For June?" Jack looked up at the ceiling. "Thirty-seven."

"That's not good enough."

"Sure it is," Joe said.

"Why?"

"It includes the first two weeks. The last two we averaged forty-five. Over forty-five."

120

"Over forty-five!" Mama said. "But, that's wonderful."

"Still, Mama. Papa wouldn't have allowed it," I said.

"Allowed what?"

"Taking in the money."

She was smiling so I would know there was no malice, and raised her eyes to the ceiling. "How do you know he didn't arrange it?"

Should she really be so flip? But now I sensed that pushing this farther would threaten the exuberance everybody felt and who wanted to do that?

"Millionaires," Jack was saying, "we're going to be millionaires." He was rubbing his index finger and thumb together. It was a gesture Mama didn't like—she said it was done by people making fun of Jews—but she laughed as she turned away to the stove.

"Mr. Rockefeller here," Aunt Esther said. She was laughing, too, her huge body shaking.

Rose and Gert were standing in the middle of the room, looking around, smiling little half-expectant smiles. They weren't sure what was going on, but they knew it was good. "So, my idea is," Joe was telling Heshie, "we ask Uncle Izzie to lend us a little more money and we buy another freezer. Because now we *know* we can pay him back. We *know* it."

Mama disappeared into the living room and came back a moment later. "The house looks very nice, Birdie. Very clean."

"Thank you," I said.

It was too late for shul, of course, but the table was ready for *Shabbes*, covered with a white tablecloth and set with the two pewter candlesticks and wine and Papa's kiddush cup, the silver goblet for sacramental wine, and while technically we should have eaten hours before, nobody seemed to care. In the middle of the tumult, Aunt Esther came in with the challah, the special twisted bread for *Shabbes*, on a plate, and we all sat down at the dining-room table.

"All right, all right," Mama said in the English she was using more and more. "I'm happy, too. But remember. Is *Shabbes*."

We quieted down. Mama lit the candles and, putting her hands over her eyes the old-fashioned way, said the prayers over them. Jack and Heshie were whispering about something. She ignored them. She picked up Papa's kiddush cup and handed it to Joe. "We use Papa's kiddush cup," she said. "Because we remember my husband, your beloved father, who gave so much to us."

As she said it, her voice broke.

Everybody grew quiet, even Rose and Gert. I half expected Joe to say he didn't want to do it, anyway, but he picked up the kiddush cup without hesitating and lifted the cup. *"Baruch atah adonai, elohaynu melech haolam. Borai pre hagofin."*

"Amen," we all said.

Behind Joe, on the table, was the postcard of Papa and Bubba.

And suddenly, hearing Joe recite a prayer Papa had recited for us hundreds of times, the house became full of him: Papa saying his prayers, rocking Gert on his toes, letting us count his change late at night when the horse had been stabled and he was home, smelling of sweat and tobacco and hay. My throat closed up and I cried so uncontrollably, just like Aunt Annie at the funeral, that I had to get up, turn my face away, and walk through the hallway to the bathroom.

*　　*　　*

Would he have come to America at all if he had known that twenty-four years later he would be dead? Would he have come to Harrisburg?

It was amazing how you decided something small and it seemed to change your whole life. A man says he's going out for some milk and he gets run over by a truck. If he'd only waited a few minutes or decided he wanted tea, he would be alive. Papa had decided we should move to Harrisburg. If he had stayed in New York, he probably wouldn't have caught a cold and he'd have been alive.

But how could you tell? You couldn't. You just had to make these decisions and hope for the best. If Papa had come to New York one year later, he wouldn't have met Mama—she would have married somebody else, and all of us would never have been born. Which meant that since he had done that, some other group of kids never *had* been born. You could almost imagine their spirits, swirling about in the air, invisible, wishing they could inhabit a body the way we did.

There was a light knock on the door. "Birdie, you're all right, *mein kind?*" It was Aunt Esther.

"Yes," I managed to say.

"I just wanted to make sure," she said gently.

Through the door it sounded quiet. They were waiting for me. I sat for a few minutes, until my tears dried. Then I went back into the kitchen. Mama was looking at me, her lips pressed close together, an older version of the picture on the table, lined where the face in the picture was smooth, hair shot through with strands of gray where it used to be coal black.

"Gut," she said. She pointed toward the bread, and to me.

"*Baruch atah adonai, elohaynu melech haolam,*

123

hamotzie lechem min haaretz," I said, barely conscious that I was saying anything, startled by the chorus of amens. I began pulling pieces of challah off and handing it around the table, big pieces because I knew everybody was hungry.

"Not so beeg."

"Okay, okay."

She was in charge! As much as I hated to admit it, she had come through. Whether it was opening the store, or giving credit, or serving "the colored," or selling ham, or closing for *Shabbes* but letting Roxanne's mother stand behind the counter, she who had never made decisions had made them all!

And now, watching her, I realized how lonely she must be. At night, instead of being able to crawl to the foot of somebody else's bed for answers the way we could, she had to have all the answers herself. She had had to hide how upset she was about the prospect of working in Uncle Max's mill, of moving back to New York, about taking money out of savings. And even when she was forced to admit something, it came with an apology.

To have to contend with all that and keep the store going! Why hadn't I seen before what an amazing thing that was!

Heshie and Jack were talking about the war. "What Wilson wants, see," Jack was saying soberly, "is that this will never happen again. See, we're the strongest country in the world. No, we *are*. These countries, see, they been knocking each other over the head for centuries. Germany. Italy. England. *Russia*. Well, us Yanks go in there, show 'em who's boss, and then we never have to fight there again."

" 'Yankee doodle went to town,' " Joe started singing, " 'a-ridin' on a pony.' "

Jack looked startled. He whirled around to see if Joe was making fun of him. But Joe kept on singing. After a beat, Jack and Heshie joined in.

" 'Yankee doodle keep it up, Yankee doodle dandy,' " we sang. And then, as we finished, Joe began singing, more slowly, another song we had learned that year in music. In fact, there had been a special assembly about the war that week, and at the end we had all sung it while teachers joined in with unusual fervor and Miss McMurtry banged it out on the piano up on the stage.

" 'Oh beautiful, for spacious skies, for amber waves of grain,' " we sang, even Gert, watching us and coming in a little late.

I looked around to see whether Mama was upset. This wasn't exactly a *Shabbes* prayer.

She wasn't in her seat, and neither was Esther. Looking through the doorway into the kitchen, I caught a glimpse of Mama's dress.

I got up and walked into the kitchen. She and Esther were standing over the stove, ladling soup into bowls.

"Can I help?"

Mama looked at me, surprised. "Don't you want to stay in there?"

"When it's time to eat," I said.

"Well, we could use the help." She handed me a bowl of soup, golden broth, the round globules of fat floating on top, full of chunks of chicken and carrot and celery, and in the middle a plump matzo ball.

"Who gets it?"

"Why don't we start with Gert this time."

She smiled at me. I smiled back. Then I turned to take the bowl into the dining room.

Finished singing, they were back to talking about the war. Heshie was explaining to Gert who exactly this President Wilson was and what he was telling the other countries: Lay down your arms, listen to us, do things our way, even in Russia.

Gert was looking at him as if he were talking Turkish. I put the bowl in front of her.

Mama and Esther came in with two bowls each. "Isn't it lucky you left Russia?" Heshie asked Mama.

"Vy?"

"Because there's no war here and we're a democracy."

"Yes, that's veddy lucky."

"We're gonna teach them a lesson over there. Really. I'm telling you," Jack said.

"It vill be that easy?"

"Hey. We're the strongest country in the world," Jack said.

"I'm glad to hear it," Mama said, laughing.

At first I thought there was a note of reproach. But she wasn't the type to make fun of us. If Jack said things would go well, she probably trusted him.

And why not? It seemed to me that on that Friday evening in June, 1917, the worst was behind us. The summer had arrived. Whatever happened in Europe, for the moment, at least, our world had become, if not safe for democracy, safe for us. Its offerings lay before us like candy behind a counter, the display window clear, the price reasonable, the colors irresistibly bright.